Love, Wylie

Text copyright © 2018 by Elisa Lorello

Published by Missouri Breaks Press, P.O. Box 50729, Billings, MT 59105

ISBN-10: 0-9986305-4-3
ISBN-13: 978-0-9986305-4-0

For Kelly, the friend I can't remember not having.

Chapter One
April

"Congratulations, Wylie," said Mom. "Your Sweet Sixteen is officially underway."

I squeezed my mother. By dressing up as Ferris's girlfriend, Sloan, complete with fringe leather jacket and a brunette wig, she complemented Dad's Ferris Bueller outfit of an argyle sweater vest over a white T-shirt, tweed pants, and boat shoes. He even shaved his mustache and allowed me to mousse up his hair.

"Thanks, Mom!" I said.

"This costume party really was a great idea," she replied. "Funny, I remember being so into the sixties during the eighties. I guess—"

"Ohmigod, I can't believe you made it!" I squealed when David and Andi entered the dining room of my uncle Frankie's restaurant. I abandoned Mom, made a beeline for them, and clasped my arms around each of their necks, practically bowling them over. "You both look SO. GOOD." David, my biological father, donned black Z. Cavariccis tucked into calf-length black suede boots, a cobalt-blue shirt, and a butter-yellow silk tie tucked into the shirt, sleeves pushed up to the elbows. His dark hair was perfectly styled, with subtle streaks of blond in the front; and holy cow, I think he even put some guyliner on. Andi cut her hair and dyed it black—not a wig—and spiked it on top. Like me, she cuffed her blue jeans at the ankles but added scrunchy white socks and black patent-leather nubucks. On top she wore a faded T-shirt that said in big, block cap, bold letters FRANKIE SAY RELAX and a houndstooth blazer with ginormous shoulder pads. Broaches and band button-pins lined the lapels of her blazer, and thin rubber bracelets coiled on her wrist, with a hot red Swatch on the other. Her makeup consisted of angled lines of bold eyeshadow, pink blush, and candy apple-red lip gloss. Nice. You'd think they would look ridiculous given their age, but no. I mean, clearly they were in costume, but they looked youthful rather than like two middle-aged adults trying to pass themselves off as young.

I extended my phone in front of us for a group selfie.

"Wylie," said Andi, smiling widely, "you look fantastic."

David concurred. "Even prettier than Boy George, which is saying a lot." He scanned the dining room. "Seriously, you did an outstanding job with your costume, and this place. Especially the MTV logo. Like taking a step back in time. All that's missing is the DeLorean."

"Thanks," I beamed. "David, you look just like that guy from that band—you know, with the video that looks like an Indiana Jones movie."

"Simon LeBon," said David. "Andi liked them when she was your age. Him especially."

Andi shot him an amused look. "That's one," she said to him, then turned to me. "We've got a bet over how many times the phrase 'when I was your age'—or some semblance of it—is uttered tonight from the adults."

"I know; my parents have already said it a zillion times," I said.

"Speaking of which, we should say hello to them," said David, his tone and demeanor changing from endearing to obligated. He excused them and they walked away, David's hand lightly resting on Andi's back.

One by one, the rest of my friends arrived, some of them having carpooled. My bestie, Roxanne Maslow, and I had spent the entire day assembling our outfits, with me doing our hair and makeup—she decided to be one of the backup singers from that "Addicted to Love" video—and she came with me to help set up. Just about every girl had some variation of leggings, oversized neon T-shirt, and teased or crimped hair. The guys I'd invited showed up in plain jeans and shirts but wore their dads' sport jackets and pushed the sleeves up. Wow. Real original. My other bestie, Bottsy—we were so used to using the nickname that I sometimes forgot his real name was John Botts—looked hilarious in a mullet wig. He hugged me and said, "Welcome to Club Sixteen, Baker. Time to start paying dues."

"What are the dues?" I asked.

He pointed to his cheek. "I'll settle on a kiss for now."

I rolled my eyes and pecked him on the cheek just as Hillary Griffin and Christina Dickerson entered. Hillary did the leggings-baggy shirt-teased hair thing. Christina wore a see-through white lace top over a black bra, a denim miniskirt over lace stockings, and granny boots. She also over-moussed her blonde hair. I don't know whether she achieved Madonna; more like a fashion-blind hooker caught in the rain. I had wavered on whether to invite them. Lately Christina had been treating Roxanne and me as if she were doing us a favor by hanging out with us. But my sister Trish told me that someone like that would probably make a big stink about not getting invited.

I barely got in a hello when Christina responded with, "Ohmigod, who is that?" as she spied on David, watching him shake my dad's hand, both of them looking stiff and polite. Seeing them dressed up so silly, yet looking so serious and awkward, was a strange sight. "He looks like a celebrity."

I instantly regretted inviting Christina. And Hillary, by default.

"Oh, he's, um…he and his wife are close friends of the family,"

I stammered. None of my friends, with the exception of Roxanne and Bottsy, knew about David being my biological father. I didn't mind people knowing—despite the weirdness of it all, there was also something cool about it—but my mom and David were both adamant on keeping it a secret, and for the first time, I could see why. It would be hard to explain the complicated story without unloading a lot of family baggage.

Hillary tilted her chin to get a better look. "What's his name?"

"His name is David, and hers is Andi." I hadn't properly prepared to deal with questions about David and Andi, mostly because I didn't think any of my friends would give a shit-fritter about any grown-ups in the room.

"He. Is. *Hot.*"

Eiw. I did not like the way Christina said that.

"Um, Christina, that's like, my dad you're ogling—I mean, he might as well be. He's the same age."

Christina rolled her eyes around. "Whatever, Baker." Then she finally noticed me. "So who are you supposed to be?"

"Boy George," I replied.

"You dressed as a *guy*?"

"It's called gender-bending. Everyone in the eighties did it."

She looked at me as if I was the one who invented the practice, and then aimed her phone at David, zooming in on his face.

"What are you doing?" I asked.

"Oh, come on. He is too hot not to get a pic. And just think, if he's this gorgeous now, imagine what he looks like in normal clothes."

I wanted to take her phone and stomp on it, tell her that her sneaking snapshots of David somehow made *me* feel violated, but I had more guests to greet.

Sixteen of the twenty guests I invited had showed. Trish, dressed in a school uniform as one of *The Facts of Life* girls (I did *her* hair and makeup too!), also invited a couple of her friends, and of course, my parents, my uncle Frankie and aunt Jill, my younger cousins Jon and Stephen, and my other aunt and uncle on my dad's side. The dance floor was occupied at all times, with no one seeming to miss any Katy Perry or Lorde or Bruno Mars songs. Uncle Frankie dimmed the lights and used the DJ strobes to create that cool stop-motion effect. We looked like a kaleidoscope, some kind of neo-cubist painting come to life. I thought about how I might capture it on canvas.

We took a break to eat and happily stuffed ourselves thanks to a buffet of pasta, sliders, herb-crusted salmon, chicken and mashed potatoes, mixed veggies, and salad between endless chatter. The restaurant staff, dressed in normal black pants and white shirts, manned the buffet stations and helped with service, each one wishing me a happy birthday as I made my way down the line. I am not going to lie—I loved all the attention. When I got to the sliders, I could have sworn the guy behind the sterno winked at me. He wore wire-rimmed glasses.

"Hey, Wylie," he said. As if we already knew each other.

It was like I was struck dumb for a second. Confused.

Did I know him? He looked familiar... but from where? When?

"Um, hi," I said, but by then he was smiling and serving the next guest in line. I spied the three-row silver-studded black leather bracelet he was wearing on his left wrist. It fit in with the décor.

Next thing I knew, my eyes followed from wrist to elbow, white-cuffed sleeve sloppily rolled around it, to shoulder, to the mop of hair that had a little bit of a Beck vibe, with long bangs that he had to shake out of his eyes without using his hands. He looked *very* familiar. About Trish's age. The lighting was too dim to catch any more detail.

That bracelet, though. Cool.

"Get a move on, Boy George," said Bottsy as he playfully pushed me down the line.

The slider server didn't look at me again.

I carried my plate from table to table to make sure I was properly mingling with all my guests, something my mother had reminded me to do. I even introduced Roxanne and Bottsy to David and Andi.

"It's nice to finally put some faces to names," said David.

"Same here," said Bottsy, who quickly added, "I'm wearing a wig."

"I figured that," said David.

I burst out laughing, and Bottsy's face went crimson. As we walked back to our table, Bottsy said, "Take me out back and shoot me. Your biological dad thinks I'm a moron."

"Oh, stop. He does not. And what do you care? It's not like you're going to work for him."

"I care what your family thinks of me, Wylie."

"I think it's sweet," said Roxanne.

It had only been seven months since David and I found out we were father and daughter. I still needed to wrap my head around thinking of David and Andi as family, even though I most certainly wanted all of us to be.

"Aw, Bottsy. Of course it's sweet," I said. We set our plates on the table and were about to sit, when Bottsy suggested we go someplace less crowded.

"Like where?" I asked.

"I don't know. Just… away from all the people."

I caught Roxanne frowning, and then rolling her eyes around, from the corner of my eye.

"It's a *party*, Botts. In fact, it's *my* party. It would be rude to duck out of my own party when everyone is eating."

"You're right," he said. "I guess I'm just still embarrassed."

"Well, you have nothing to be embarrassed about. Let's eat."

After I finished eating, I went to the restroom. Hillary, Christina, and

Caitlyn Kelley were touching up their makeup and raising the height of their hair with portable combs and hair spray. Caitlyn handed me her comb. "Help me, Wylie." I sectioned off her hair and teased it like a madwoman. Just as I finished, Andi entered the restroom, her face shiny.

"Hey," she said. "Having a good time?"

Christina and Hillary exchanged a smirk, directed a catty smile at Andi, and left the restroom with Caitlyn dawdling behind them. Andi looked at the door where they'd exited, as if they were still there, then at me, as if to say, *WTF?*

I shook my head and shrugged. "Whatever."

Andi repeated her question.

"Totally," I said. "You?"

Her green eyes sparkled. "I am having a *wonderful* time. I know this probably sounds like crazy midlife crisis talk, but this is the Sweet Sixteen party I always wanted."

I had no idea what "crazy midlife crisis talk" was, but I figured it had to do with the fact that when I'd first told Andi about the theme of my party, she told me about how for her Sweet Sixteen, in lieu of a party, she'd invited a few friends to the movies and then out for ice cream. "I don't know why. I guess I didn't think I was worthy of a party at the time," she'd said.

I washed and dried my hands and leaned with my back to the sink counter, watching Andi dab her nose with a compact powder pad. "So, is that the way you and David used to dress in high school?" I asked.

"Something like that. I was really into the sixties back then."

"Ohmigod, so was my mom!" The idea that Andi had something in common with my mother was strange. They weren't exactly the best of friends.

"And I didn't know David back then, but I've seen pictures of him from that time, and he didn't look much different."

"So, would you, like, have had a crush on him if you knew him back then?"

She made a swooning face. "Without a doubt."

"My friends Christina and Hillary—the ones who were just in here—think he's hot." I made a gagging face, checked underneath the stalls to make sure we were alone, and dropped the volume of my voice even though we were. "I know they don't know he's my real dad, but it's so weird to have any of my friends think that."

Andi laughed. "David is what my friends and I would've described during the eighties as 'a total fox'." She added after a beat, "Sorry, does it bother you when I say things like that?"

"No, I *expect* it from you. You're *married* to him."

She watched my reflection as I re-applied my purple lipstick. "I can't believe how lucky I am," she said. The way she said it—so much *gratitude*—made me stop what I was doing and look at her.

"I'm glad he has you," I said. "No matter how many times I've tried to picture him with my mom, I just can't." It wasn't that I wanted my mom and David to be together. More like trying to picture what my life would have been like with my biological parents and not the jumbled mess finding him had turned my family life into.

Andi took hold of me and held me tight. I had no idea what prompted it, if it was a happy hug or a sad hug or what, but when she finally let go her eyes were misted over. "Well," she said, taking hold of the ends of my cornrow braids and evening them out, "let's get back to the dance floor. Everybody Wang Chung tonight," she added, deadpan.

"What does that even mean?" I asked.

"Beats the shit out of me," she said, before gasping and covering her mouth, and both of us breaking into a laugh. I love when Andi slips and curses in front of me. She gets so self-conscious. I think it's because she's an English professor. David told me she has no qualms about cursing at home, though. We walked out arm and arm until we were in eyeshot of my mom.

One of the slower songs, "Save a Prayer," came up on the playlist. My friends wandered off the dance floor and were just kind of hanging out around the perimeter, but David escorted Andi to the middle of the floor, took hold of her arms, and gently pulled them to his shoulders before wrapping his arms delicately around her waist. He was much taller than she, yet that didn't seem to faze either of them. I was fixated throughout the duration of the song—couldn't take my eyes off them not taking their eyes off each other, as if they were not only the lone couple on the dance floor but also in the entire restaurant.

Thing is, as I looked at him—at *them*—I could kind of see what Christina and the others saw. It wasn't his looks, though. It was his *presence*, the way he carried himself. As if he really was someone famous. Like they were some kind of power couple. Of all the times I've seen my parents together—even tonight—they've *never* looked at each other the way David and Andi do, and not just right then and there on the dance floor. My parents never expressed that kind of affection—David's hand resting light as a feather on Andi's back, holding hands in public, a caress of the wrist.

And then, like magnets, their lips met each other. So soft and gentle and romantic.

"She doesn't even, like, have a good body," said Christina, breaking my focus. "What is he doing with *her*?"

The sudden realization that all my friends were standing there, gawking at them right along with me, ruined the moment.

I whipped around and faced them. "That's really rude, Dickerson," I snapped. "How would you like it if I came to your party and trash-talked one of your guests behind their back?"

Christina's cheeks turned pink as she glared at me.

"So who are they, anyway?" asked my friend Annette. "Are they related to you?"

The song ended, replaced by something more upbeat, and David and Andi left the dance floor while Trish and her friends took over. I was so preoccupied with wanting to preserve the picture of them, savor the moment, that I hadn't realized I nodded my head in response to Annette's question.

"You said they were *friends* of the family, not *actual* family," said Hillary, eager to catch me in a lie. "Which is it?"

"Haven't you ever had an aunt or uncle or a cousin who weren't your blood relatives but were so close you treated them like they were?" I said, hoping that would cover my tracks.

"Because you kind of look like him," said Annette. "I saw him up close before when we were at the buffet table, and he kind of makes the same facial expressions as you do."

I was used to people in the know telling me how much David and I resembled each other, especially our eyes. Almost like cat's eyes, with dark lashes. I still remember seeing him for the first time at his house in Northampton, Massachusetts, and feeling as if I'd just looked into some kind of crazy funhouse mirror that shows you what you would look like as the opposite sex, and older too. But in a way it had also been validating. Even before I knew my stepdad wasn't my biological father, I somehow knew something made us different. I would pore through old photographs, trying to find a resemblance, a similar mannerism or personality quirk, something to connect us—a shared hobby or favorite movie—and come up short.

In fact, that's why I'd confronted my mom before finally finding David; I'd been convinced that they'd adopted me, that even she wasn't my real mom.

But Annette's recognition made me nervous rather than appreciative. I didn't think anyone would notice with me wearing so much makeup.

"Yeah, right," I said to Annette, as if to blow her off and dismiss the notion as absurd.

"He is rather good-looking despite the cheesy costume," said Caitlyn.

"I would so completely do him," said Christina. "Married or not."

Now I was downright skeeved out. "Do you know how old he is?" I asked, not waiting for an answer. "He's *old*. Like, almost *fifty*. You'd do a fifty-year-old? That is just completely gross."

The girls' mouths dropped open at this information. "No *way*," they said simultaneously.

"I thought he was like, thirty-five tops," said Caitlyn.

"Which is still too old," I countered.

"How old is *she*?" asked Hillary, referring to Andi.

"I'm not sure," I said. "Like, forty-five, I think?"

"That explains the muffin top," said Christina.

"Where do you see a muffin top?" I said. "She's wearing a big T-shirt and an oversized jacket with shoulder pads. You cannot tell a single thing about her body based on her clothes. Besides, who *cares*? She's a cool person."

"All right, all right already," said Christina. "What are you so defensive about?"

"Because you're being *rude*. Andi is my friend and my guest, and if you keep it up, I will ask you to leave. I mean it, Dickerson, I will."

Christina huffed and rolled her eyes around. "Fine. You know, this party is really lame. Who's coming with me to the Ladies?" Caitlyn and Hillary opted to go, and I turned away from them. David and Andi had not only left the dance floor, but also the dining room. I was about to look for them when Bottsy blocked my path. "Let's dance," he said, taking my hand.

"Not now," I said, pulling my hand free. I hadn't meant to be so abrupt in doing so. "Sorry."

"Where are you going?' asked Roxanne as I brushed passed her without answering. I found David and Andi in a dim corner of the lobby, near the coat-check room. They were huddled close together in a clandestine sort of way. He looked as if he was about to kiss her. I wasn't even sure what to say to them.

Just then my parents entered the lobby. "We've been looking for you," Mom said to me. "It's time for cake."

David and Andi looked at us as if we'd just caught them rummaging through people's wallets or something. "You weren't leaving, were you?" I asked.

"Of course not," he said. "We just came out for some air."

"Me too," I said.

We all headed back to the dining room, where I gathered everyone around to the cake—a Rubik's Cube in mid-twist. My parents had surprised me with it, and it looked *amazing*. My friends and I took a bunch of pictures. I hugged my parents and thanked them profusely. "Ohmigod, I *love* it! I almost don't want to cut into it!" They knew I'd say that.

Wish time.

I had been thinking all day about what to wish for. I mean, so you're sixteen—big deal. It doesn't change the fact that you're still stuck in high school with a face that looks like a golf course full of divots. It doesn't change the fact that you can't legally drink, vote, or drive a car. It doesn't change the fact that Ryan Gosling doesn't know I'm alive.

I'd wanted to wish for something meaningful, that would somehow affect me as a person—and couldn't think of a single thing. What did I *really* want? The last seven months had been a carnival ride of epic proportions—finding my biological father; my mother hating me for it; my dad trying so hard to keep the peace; the endless fights between my mother and David and Andi; Trish being super-supportive one minute (she's the one who'd helped me track him down in the first place and goaded me into meeting him), aloof the next. I still loved drawing and painting and hair and makeup and hanging with Roxanne and Bottsy. But some days I didn't know who I was or who I'd become. Who did I want to be?

I inhaled, looked up for a split second, and spotted David and Andi off to the side, him standing behind her with his armed wrapped protectively around her, her eyes glistening with a mix of contentment and sadness in the glow of the candlelight.

And then, closing my eyes, my hands together and interlocked my fingers, like in prayer position, the wish came to me, seemingly out of nowhere: *I want to fall in love.*

I extinguished every candle in one breath and basked in the applause, as if they all somehow heard my wish and their clapping affirmed approval of my choice. I looked up, and there, leaning against the wall, was the boy with the bracelet, grinning and nodding his head. As if he knew exactly what I'd wished for.

Chapter Two

Turning sixteen had no effect on my return to Gerald Ford High School on Monday morning. The walls were the same blinding yellow (supposedly to stimulate creativity; more like it stimulated glaucoma); the floors the same dirty pseudo-linoleum; the classrooms the same ancient fixtures, sealed windows, soul-draining fluorescent lighting, and teachers talking about nothing but tests. I don't know why I'd expected change. I thought maybe I'd suddenly feel more like a professional or something. Like I'd start dressing in pantsuits and carrying a briefcase instead of a backpack.

Christina joined Roxanne, Caitlyn, and me for lunch, which immediately aroused my suspicion given that Christina usually skips lunch and walks around the track instead. She pulled out a plastic baggie of carrot and celery sticks and bit into one.

"So?" she said, as if waiting impatiently while she crunched.

I stared at her blankly. "What?"

"When are you going to tell us who the mystery man at your party *really* was, and when are we going to see what he looks like in normal clothes?"

"I told you who he was. A friend of the family. And he looks exactly the same, only he doesn't tuck any part of his clothes into any other part of his clothes other than his dress shirts."

"I think he was wearing eyeliner too," said Caitlyn.

"Whatever," I said. "It was a *costume party*. He doesn't wear eyeliner in real life either, OK?"

"What did he give you for your birthday?" asked Christina.

"A couple of art books." One of Keith Haring and one of Patrick Nagel, to be exact. Two prominent pop artists from the eighties, both of whom died tragically young.

Christina scrunched her face as if she'd just bitten into a rotten carrot. "Why?"

I, in turn, widened my eyeballs and made a face to imply she was stupid. "Um, because I like art? Look, why do you even care?" I asked. "He's more than twice your age, he's married, and I doubt he'd talk to you for more than five minutes even if you paid him to."

She trapped me in a death stare before saying, "I want my gift back."

"Excuse me?"

She annunciated each word slowly through clenched teeth. "I want you to give me back the gift I gave you."

"It's rude to ask someone for their gift back, Dickerson," I said. "Honestly, don't you have any manners at all?"

"You are such a bitch, Wylie," she said. "Not to mention a total loser. I don't even know why I even went to your lame-ass oldies party."

I balled my hands into fists under the table. "You disrespected my family friends, said lewd things about them not only behind my back but *to my face*, asked for your stupid birthday present back, and you're calling *me* a bitch?"

Christine stood up. "Oh, we are so done," she said, followed by, "You should know better than to cross me."

"Who are *you*?" I said.

She gave me one last death glare, the kind that comes with invisible lasers that really do bore a hole into your skin, and I knew that was the declaration of war. Furthermore, I knew that I was going to have to watch my back from here on out. Roxanne's worried expression confirmed it.

The first time Andi came to tutor me for English had ended up being a disaster, with Mom forbidding Andi from having anything to do with me. (Hello, Overreaction? This is Janine Baker, Wylie's mom.) But eventually Mom eased up, and we agreed to do a bi-weekly Skype session instead of Andi driving out here to West Hartford or Mom driving me to David and Andi's home in Massachusetts. Plus I didn't want to give up my Saturdays for schoolwork if I didn't have to, even though working with Andi didn't always feel like schoolwork. I wished I were old enough to take one of her college classes.

Tonight I didn't have much other than an essay due the next day, and I had already worked on a few drafts with Andi, sending them back and forth via email.

"You're more or less good to go with this," she said. Her hair was less spiky than it was at the party, and she was makeup-free. "Just some proofreading errors. Hopefully your teacher will agree."

"I cannot wait to be done with high school," I said for the gazillionth time. "It's just so...*pointless*."

"It shouldn't be," said Andi, also for the gazillionth time. "That's the sad part."

"I just want *out* already. And not just high school. I want out of this high school. And West Hartford and Connecticut."

"Where would you want to go?"

I shrugged. "I don't know." I changed the subject. "So my friend— or rather my *ex*-friend, Christina—totally hates me now."

"What happened?" asked Andi.

"She said some rude and inappropriate things about David, and when I called her out on it, she got mad and pretty much declared war on me."

"Wylie, that's terrible." She added, "Does your mom know?"

"What could *she* do?"

"You should tell her."

I waved my hand in a dismissive motion. "Christina Dickerson is drama-obsessed. She'll move on to someone or something else next week. I think she was jealous because someone other than her got all the attention for a night."

"Just promise you'll let someone know if things get out of hand. Especially David. He wants to be kept in the loop where your life is concerned."

"I know," I said. "I will."

I put my elbows on the desk, leaning lazily. "You should've seen all the pictures from the party my friends posted. And, um, you should probably tell David that there are now, like, a ton of pictures of him dressed like an eighties music video star floating all over Facebook."

Andi laughed and then caught herself. "I shouldn't be laughing—David is so not going to like that. And not just because of the way he's dressed."

"Why is he so squeamish about having his picture taken?"

"He has no problem with having his picture taken. It's having said pictures floating all over the Internet that he doesn't like, although in this day and age it's unavoidable." She paused, as if to choose her words carefully. "I guess he's trying to hold on to the illusion of privacy."

I knew David was in another line of work before he became an art dealer, but neither he, Andi, nor my parents would specifically state what he did other than "sales." I knew he even went by a different name—*Devin*. In fact, the first time my mother saw him in at least fifteen years, she called him by that name. And Andi constantly calls him "Dev," which he doesn't seem to mind, although woe to anyone else who dared to.

"Andi, why are you and David and my mom always so secretive about his past? I really want to know."

"It's complicated," said Andi. "I know I've said that before, and I know it's a copout, but David was a different person back then, and it's a part of himself he no longer wants to be or share."

"A lot of people at the party asked how David and I were related—or rather, *if* we were related. I wasn't expecting that. I mean, I was all dressed up and honestly didn't think anyone would see the resemblance."

"The eyes tell all," she said.

"Well, I didn't tell anyone the truth. I mean, I told them he's a friend of the family, which isn't a total lie, right?"

"There's enough truth there," she said.

"And honestly, what's the big deal?"

Rather than answer my question, Andi hastily wrapped things up, saying she needed to do some editing. After we ended our session, I proofread my essay and printed it out, finished the rest of my homework, and texted with Bottsy, thanking him again for the charm bracelet. He could only afford one charm, but it was perfect: a paint palette.

I stared at the Google homepage on my laptop for a moment before typing my biological father's name into the search box when my phone alerted me to a text from Caitlyn. She sent me two screenshots of Christina's Facebook page. The first was of her status update, which read:

Wylie Baker is a Loser.

Seeing that ten people had hit "like" on it made my stomach lurch, but not nearly as much as the candid of David at my party did, with a caption:

Who is David Santino?

Holy crap on a cracker, how did Christina find out his last name?

Chapter Three

The next day at school, I spotted Christina in the cafeteria yet again and confronted her. "What is this weird obsession you have with David?" I asked. "Seriously, it's creepy."

Christina smirked. "What's 'creepy' is *your* obsession with him. You've spent more time defending him than most girls defend their boyfriends. And it occurred to me that maybe you don't want me talking about doing him because *you* want to."

You know when people joke that they just threw up in their mouth a little? Well, I did. For real.

I picked up Christina's can of Diet Coke and poured it over her head. Bottsy and Roxanne, who'd just arrived, gasped. The surrounding lunch table-dwellers laughed and some even applauded me as Christina shrieked, beads of Coke dripping down her face and into her eyes and from the ends of her hair. I set the can down and was about to turn on my heel when she grabbed me by my shirtsleeve and tried to smack my face. Before the violence could escalate— and really, I didn't want to resort to a catfight—one of the faculty chaperones instantly materialized, pulled the two of us apart and, with a tight grip on each of our arms, walked us to the office of Mr. Berger, the second assistant principal and disciplinarian.

———

We sat in Berger's waiting room forever, silent except for the clicking keyboards from the secretaries' desks and an occasional telephone ring. On the other side of the main entrance, the bustle of switching classes had commenced without us. Mr. Berger's door remained closed, and I could hear him occasionally respond to whomever he was conversing with via telephone. Putrid, rust-hued paint peeled from the walls, and seating consisted of the knuckle-breaking metal monstrosities that were all attached to one another, rendering them immovable. The only artwork on the walls consisted of portraits of former assistant principal/disciplinarians—like a lineage of dictators. And for some reason, the place smelled like pickles.

An empty chair separated Christina and me like an invisible wall. She sobbed and dabbed at her hair with custodial brown paper towels while I stared at my purple high-top Chucks. I was in trouble. I knew I was going to get detention for this. Possibly even suspension. Plus I was going to have to call at least one of my parents, and they were going to have to find out why I'd behaved so immaturely.

Who to call—Mom or Dad?

The door opened and Mr. Berger emerged. Without addressing either of us by name, he directed us into his private office. I'd never been there before. Aesthetically speaking, it was about as impressive as the outer office. His desk was positioned in front of a picture window in need of cleaning. (What's the point of having an office with a window if your back is always to it? Then again, the Gerald Ford High School parking lot wasn't exactly a scenic view). A Grumpy Cat poster with the caption Is It Friday Yet? was Scotch-taped above the stone-age filing cabinet that would split your skull open if you were pushed into it. Really? That's your choice of artwork? We have award-winning art students in our school. And who still kept paper records? Mr. Berger, that's who. He had two manila folders in front of him—presumably ours, which he peered at before finally making eye contact with us.

"Since I don't recognize either of your names or faces, I assume this is your first major infraction," he said.

Christina and I were forced to sit in closer proximity this time, given that there were only two wooden chairs and a broken swivel chair in the room. A bed of nails would be more comfortable.

I nodded my head sheepishly. Christina continued to sob. Please.

"Sooo…" He looked at the file again, and up at Christina. "You're Christina Dickerson?" She nodded and sobbed. "Why don't you tell me what happened," he said to her.

"I was just minding my own business at lunch when Wylie came up, accused me of something despicable, and then poured my can of soda on my head. I didn't do *anything*—and she's supposed to be my *friend*!" she whined.

I resisted bellowing a loud *HA!* Don't hold out for that Golden Globe, honey.

Mr. Berger looked at me. "Wylie?"

I straightened my posture and cleared my throat. "Christina has been cyberbullying me and I demanded that she stop doing it. *She* is the one who made despicable—no, *disgusting*—remarks, prompting me to do what I did. Then she grabbed me and slapped me." Before he could respond, I added, "I know what I did was immature, but it's the culmination of a week's worth of provocation." Andi would love that I used the words *culmination* and *provocation* in the same sentence. I was already brushing up on vocabulary for next year's PSATs.

Christina's waterworks magically disappeared. "I have *not* been cyberbullying her. She's not even a Facebook friend, so how could she possibly know what I've been posting?" She glowered at me when Mr. Berger looked away.

"Are you really going with that lie when I can just pull it up on my phone right now?" I said to Christina. "Plus, you know, witnesses. I have plenty of friends who are Facebook friends with you. They take screenshots. What are you going to do, unfriend me and every mutual friend we have?"

Christina must have forgotten where she was because she threatened, "No, I'm going to make it so that you have no friends left."

Mr. Berger stepped in. "Now, hold on. What started this?"

Neither of us volunteered an answer.

"Girls, we're not going anywhere until I get to the bottom of this."

Still no takers.

Mr. Berger looked at me. "Wylie?"

Shit-fritters.

I wanted to punch that smirk off Christina's face.

I sucked in my breath. "I hosted a Sweet Sixteen costume party this past Saturday." God, it already sounded lame. "Christina was there, and made inappropriate comments about one of my guests, an adult friend of my family. She also insulted his wife behind her back. When I told her it was inappropriate, she went, like, all mental. Since then she's posted photos of this person on Facebook without his or my permission, publicly called me a loser, and is invading this family friend's privacy by using Facebook to get information about him."

Christina pounced. "That is *not* what happened. Wylie got all overprotective of this 'family friend' "—she used such a smarmy, exaggerated tone whenever she said the phrase—"when I showed concern about the nature of their relationship. I worried that this man was taking advantage of her. And *she* is the one who attacked *me* today."

"WOW," I said, flabbergasted. "That is like, more than a lie. It's bad fiction."

"I don't see any evidence of bullying," said Mr. Berger. What an assclown.

"I can show you the screenshots," I said. *I'll bet he doesn't even know what a screenshot is, the old fart.* "Heck, I can show you the actual post."

"You're both aware of the school's anti-bullying policy. That includes cyberbullying."

"And you're enforcing it so well," I said.

Mr. Berger shot me a glare in response to my sarcasm. "Consider this a warning to you both. We take bullying seriously. We also don't tolerate childish behavior in the cafeteria or anywhere else, Wylie, and for that you're going to get one day of detention."

Christina grinned victoriously, making me not only want to dump another can of Coke on her, but also follow it up with a bucket of battery acid.

"Wait—Bitchella McBitcherson here cyberbullies *and* slaps me, and *I* get a day's detention for messing up her hair?" I said.

Mr. Berger shot a second glare. "Do you want to make it two?"

I pressed my lips together and swallowed hard, forcing the tears threatening to emerge to go back to wherever they came from.

He looked at Christina. "Whatever you've been doing online, it ends now."

Christina nodded her head. "Yes, sir," she said in a patronizing voice. *Yes, sir?* Please.

"You're both suspended from school for the rest of the day, and will take the consequences for any work you miss. It's time for me to call your parents and have them come pick you up, and we're going to explain to them what happened."

This is hell. I'm burning in hell right this minute, and for no good reason.

Twenty minutes later my mother showed up, attired in the very kind of black pantsuit and black flats I'd weirdly envisioned myself wearing to school from now on. Occasionally she wore skirts, but she never looked comfortable in them. If she had it her way, she'd be an administrative assistant wearing jeans and cotton jerseys. Her hair was in need of a touch-up, gray roots sprouting from her part and fusing into the auburn color she'd been dying it lately. She wore thick black eyeliner and mascara, a look I used to like and had copied since she'd permitted me to wear makeup, until Trish gave me Bobbi Brown's makeup manual for Christmas. Since then I'd noticed that it made Mom look older than younger. I wasn't about to tell her that, though.

Christina's mother—a creepy carbon copy of Christina—just so happened to walk in right behind Mom. Mr. Berger attempted to explain the "squabble," as he called it, and suggested our moms "keep us apart" from now on.

"I don't understand," said Christina's mother to her daughter. "Didn't you just go to Wylie's party last weekend?"

Christina attempted to turn on the waterworks again. "I don't know what happened," she said. "I thought we were friends."

This time Christina's mother glared at me. "Well?"

Before I had a chance to answer, my mom chimed in. "Well, what? Don't gang up on my kid like that. This obviously isn't a one-sided situation. You keep an eye on your kid and I'll keep an eye on mine."

I wanted to hug my mom for sticking up for me, like when I was little and was knocked over on the playground by some rambunctious boys. Never mess with Janine Baker.

I picked up my paint-stained backpack and knockoff Louis V handbag and walked out with my mom, doing my best to avoid a gloating Christina. When we got into the car, I finally let myself burst into tears, mad at myself for letting Christina get to me, and humiliated by the punishment.

Mom leaned over and put her hand on my shoulder. "Tell me your side of the story."

I sucked in yet another breath and told her everything,

starting with the party. And I watched as her demeanor changed. "Goddammit," she said under her breath. Then she let it out. "You see? Do you see the trouble he's caused? He's still causing?"

"Mom, David didn't do anything but show up to a party that *I* invited him to."

"But that's your problem, Wylie—you don't think about the consequences of your actions. *This*! This is the consequence of your actions. This is what happens when you invite your biological father to your party. This is the result of your looking for your biological father to begin with. I told you to leave well enough alone."

Wow. So much for her support.

I turned the tables on her. "No, this is the consequence of your sleeping with a man and then not telling him he had a daughter."

Pretty sure my mother wanted to pour a can of Coke on *my* head at that moment. And then smack me. Or just skip straight to the smacking part.

She swallowed her rage. "We warned you that your inviting David and Andi could spell trouble. Could incite your friends to ask questions. Well, look what's happened. They're asking questions."

"Maybe I should answer them," I said. "Maybe I should tell them he's my biological dad."

"Wylie, you have to trust me when I tell you that you don't want to go down this road."

"What did my biological father do that is so awful? Did he get a sex-change operation? Was he a drug dealer? Did he have, like, multiple wives at the same time or something? Whatever it is, you must have known when you got involved with him. What, you're worried about how this makes *you* look?"

"Wylie, *enough*! Enough with the disrespect, and enough with you poking a stick at this land mine that is going to explode in your face."

She started the car, and just as she put it in gear, said, "You're grounded for the weekend."

"Fine," I countered. "Whatever." I took out my phone and plugged in my earbuds.

"Grounding includes no phone, starting the minute we get into the house."

"Fine," I said again.

We didn't speak for the rest of the ride home and most of the night.

When I woke up on my birthday, sixteen felt like a turning point. I felt older than I did the day before. Wiser. Maybe because you're one year closer to eighteen and freedom. I felt hopeful that the world was going to open up and welcome me into it, and that I was going to step forward knowing exactly who I was and who I wanted to be. But the thing is, you're no closer to freedom than you were at fifteen. And no one gives a shit who you are.

So far, being sixteen sucked.

Chapter Four

I had just enough time to text Roxanne and Bottsy and inform them that I'd be without my phone all weekend and about the detention on Monday. I was allowed to use my computer only for the purpose of doing homework, and only in a room where I could be monitored. I also wasn't allowed to go out all weekend. Mom called David that night, and from behind her bedroom door I could hear her yelling at him, even though I couldn't make out what she was saying. Once again, discord in the Baker house, thanks to Wylie. How David didn't hate me or want anything more to do with me following one of Mom's screaming sessions was beyond me. Made me feel worse than dirt.

Shortly after I went to my room, I heard a knock and my dad entered, dressed in his usual tan Dockers and plain button-down shirt, fine, ash-blond hair thinning at the top of his forehead and forming a widow's peak, recently shaved mustache, hazel eyes and rough skin exposed to the elements. He was a property manager and spent as much time outdoors as in.

"Hey," I said.

"Hey, kiddo," he said. "Heard you had a crappy day at school today."

"I've had a crappy week."

"Sucks, considering you had such a great time at your party." He said as he pulled out my desk chair, wheeled it up beside my bed, and sat. A ritual with him.

"I really did. It was a great party, wasn't it?" I asked, suddenly doubtful.

He nodded. "It really was. Everyone had a good time, including me and Mom."

I could feel tears creeping to the surface. Dad moved from the chair to the bed and put his arm around me, pulling me into a sideways hug.

"Dad, you know I love you, right? It's not like I prefer David to you. It's just that…" I searched for the right words and came up with none. Maybe all of this really was my fault. If I hadn't invited David and Andi to my party, I wouldn't be at war with Christina, wouldn't be suspended from school, wouldn't be punished. If only I'd left well enough alone, like Mom had told me to, and not gone looking for David in the first place. After all, how could I toss aside the dad who taught me how to ride a bicycle, helped me with geometry, and provided me with every material possession and food and comfort? How could I forgive myself for hurting him like that, and yet keep right on hurting him?

"I wanted them at the party," I shamefully confessed. "And I knew they wanted to be there."

"Wylie, they're your family. You don't have to explain or justify your love for them. And it doesn't change the fact that I will always love you like my own daughter. I also know you love me and I appreciate your telling me."

Despite his reassuring tone, the sadness that had dimmed his irises every time the subject of David came up, like clouds covering sunshine, settled in once again and rained guilt on me. What was it that Andi had said? *The eyes reveal all.*

"Mom always makes me feel like I have to. Mom blames me for this."

Like I wasn't to blame all along...

"Mom is afraid of your getting hurt."

"I'm hurt *now*," I said. "And she's mad at me for it. But I can't help it. He's my biological father, and I can't ever go back and pretend like I never knew that. And what Christina said just made me so mad and so sick."

"Sweetheart," he started, "she doesn't want to lose you."

"How many times do I have to tell her she's not going to?"

And just like that, we were right back to where we always were: nowhere.

It took a good five to ten seconds for either of us to put another thought together.

"Ford High School sucks," I finally blurted.

"It'll get easier when you're older and out of high school," he said.

"What if I don't want to wait?" I hopped off my bed and pulled a printout from a pile of papers on my desk. "I found out about a school where I can pick and choose whatever I want to learn, on my own schedule. If all I want to learn is basket-weaving, then all they'll teach me is basket-weaving."

I wasn't about to tell him that I'd learned about the school from Andi sometime last month. I'd been complaining to her about how pointless memorizing a bunch of dates in European history was for an art major, when she mentioned it. "I don't know if it's a better way to be educated, but it certainly is a fascinating model," she'd said, talking to me as if I were one of her fellow teachers, or even one of her college students. She never even realized she put the bug in my head.

He stared at the pages, presumably reading. "And how does that prepare you for college?"

"OK, so maybe I used a stupid example. The point is that I read all about it and the kids actually go to college knowing exactly what they want to do, and have the focus and concentration to handle the demands of college."

"Where is this school?"

I braced myself. "Massachusetts."

He pounded the bed and stood up, towering over me. "No."

"You didn't let me finish, Dad. The original school is in Massachusetts, but they have other schools that copy their model all over, including one right here in Connecticut."

"Wylie, one of the reasons why your mother and I moved here was to make sure you got a good education. Now you want to go somewhere else just because you got into a fight with one of your friends? To Massachusetts?"

Yet another one who didn't get it.

"It's not just that. I'm sick of being bored all the time, of ugly walls and pointless lessons and teachers who want to be there about as much as we do. I'm sick of doing all this work and studying and not *learning* anything. I'm sick of this town and seeing the same faces day in and day out."

Dad pushed the chair back under the desk. "I'm sorry for what happened today, and I understand why you reacted the way you did, but it was still wrong and you're still grounded." Before he closed the door behind him, he uttered one last apology: "I'm sorry none of this is enough for you."

His words struck me in the gut with the force of a kettle bell.

Why couldn't it be enough? Why had meeting David and Andi not filled a hole but dug an even deeper one? Ever since I'd met David, West Hartford was more like a typical town with nothing to offer other than the standards—parks and shopping centers and movie theatres. Hartford was a joke compared to cities like Boston and New York. The first time I officially visited David and Andi in

Northampton, they'd taken me to the town of Amherst, and we walked up and down Main Street. And while it boasted the same things as West Hartford, it had a different feel to it—*bohemian*, Andi called it. The kind of place you could build a life if you were an artist or a writer. Even the poet Emily Dickinson had lived there.

What if I was meant to be there instead? With every day that passed, Ford High School and West Hartford were places where everyone spoke the same language but me.

And yet, I didn't think I fit into David and Andi's world any more than I fit into my own. I wanted what they had—they were their own bosses and traveled whenever they wanted. They knew things about art and literature and loved to share those things with others. My parents didn't share their passions with me—I didn't even know if they had any passions other than football season. They occasionally ranted about the way the country was being run, but other than that, they didn't seem to have an opinion on anything. It's not like they didn't teach me anything—my mom taught me how to make baked ziti and how to defend myself against an attacker; Dad taught me how to save money; both Mom and Dad taught me about being polite to others; Trish taught me how to apply liquid eyeliner in one smooth line and how to do word problems in math. Those things all became a part of me. So why didn't I feel like me when I was around them anymore?

At what point do you get to control your own fate? At what point do teachers and parents stop making decisions for you? At what point do your friends stop measuring themselves up to you, and vice versa? At what point does love mean something? Eighteen? Twenty-one? Because all this supervision and social construct of rules felt like a noose around my neck.

Late at night, after everyone went to bed, I crept into my sister's room, swiped her phone from beside her night table, went back to my room and texted Andi as fast as I could:

Suspended from school. Punished at home. Ex-friend bashing me on Facebook. Parents hate me. No one understands. HELP! Love, Wylie

I stealthily returned Trish's phone.

Two days later on Sunday, during my allotted (and supervised, ugh) computer time for homework, I found an email from Andi with an attachment of a PDF file, titled "Letter from Birmingham Jail."

Dear Wylie-
David told me about what happened at school. Here's something to keep you occupied while you're grounded. Please read and annotate it like I taught you.
Hugs, Andi

Seriously? I reach out to you, and you assign me *homework*? What the hell? I thought she'd at least give me some advice or commiserate or something.

I didn't bother to download the document. Didn't even reply to Andi. Why bother? Apparently she didn't get me either.

Chapter Five

After the final bell rang on Monday, I reported to the art room (it turned out that's where detention was), my stomach doing flip-flops as I wondered whom I'd be serving time with. I'd already seen *The Breakfast Club*. Yeah, so not real.

The room was larger than most classrooms, dominated by four square-shaped, paint-splattered wooden tables and accompanying swivel chairs; the easels and supply closets filled up the rest. Typically, when we spent class time painting, we pushed the tables against the wall and moved the easels in their place during class, then moved the furniture back five minutes before the end-of-class bell.

I took my usual seat at the far left table and looked at the paintings-in-progress on the easels lined up against the back wall. Mine was off to the side—a still life—half-finished. I hoped I'd be allowed to work on it for the next two hours.

Cecil Jamison, Ford's star athlete, sauntered in wearing his varsity letterman jacket showcasing the school's hideous maroon and marigold colors, workout pants, and sunglasses.

Colin Furman, class pothead, followed him in greasy denim jacket and matching jeans.

Geez. Maybe this *was* the Breakfast Club. Who was I—the princess, or the basket case?

Don't answer that.

One more student entered the room. He wore clean blue jeans and a slick black leather biker jacket. His hair, the color of burnt umber mixed with black—like dark roast coffee—was styled in unruly layers and covered his ears.

Oh. My God. It was the slider guy at my party. The one who winked at me. The one who watched me as I made my wish.

He made eye contact with me through the same wire-rim glasses he wore at the party (his eyes were cerulean blue, perhaps mixed with a little cobalt; I could see them better now) and raised his eyebrows, but I pretended not to see him. Rather, I tried and failed. He sat at one of the front tables, but then changed his mind a few seconds later, headed straight for my table, and slid into the swivel chair across from me.

"Hey, Wylie," he said, exactly the same way he did that night.

"Hey," I replied, as confused as ever.

"You don't know me, do you," he said.

"You were one of the servers at my uncle's restaurant where I had my Sweet Sixteen party."

"But you don't know my name."

"Should I?"

He leaned across the table and extended his hand out, palm up. "Clark Anderson." What did he want, a tip? Uncertain of the gesture, I took a guess and meekly slapped him five. Apparently I'd made the right call, because he withdrew his hand in satisfaction.

"I'm Wylie," I said and cringed. *He already knows your name, dumbass.*

He smiled rather than call out my dumbassery. "Wylie what?"

"Wylie Baker."

"You a junior?" he asked.

I laughed at the notion. "Soph. You?"

"Senior."

"That explains why I've never seen you before the party," I said.

"Actually, we're in the same study hall," he replied.

My jaw dropped. "Really?"

"When I'm there I sit in the back, but I'm almost never there, which is why I'm here," he said with an amiable smile. I smiled back. *So that's why he looked familiar!*

"Were you there today?" I asked.

He nodded. "First time in weeks. So what are you in for, Wylie Baker? Cool name, by the way," he added.

"Thanks," I said, and then answered his question. "I sort of got into a fight."

He raised his eyebrows again. "Really? You don't look like the war-mongering type."

"I dumped a can of Diet Coke on my ex-friend's head."

He laughed. "I don't even know her, and I'm sure she deserved it."

"Oh, she totally deserved it. And she got off scot-free. She didn't even have to spend the rest of the day at school with Coke-infused hair."

"That blows," he said.

His eyes twinkled when he smiled. And I got a tingling sensation when they did.

At that moment my English teacher, Mr. Fischetti, who looked a little like the actor Steve Carrell, entered the room with a stack of papers and looked around as if he'd never been there before.

"Mr. Fish!" said Clark. "What did you do to get sent here?"

Mr. Fischetti looked at Clark as if they were old friends. "My number came up in the rotation." He dropped the papers onto Mrs. Howard's desk and pulled a sheet from the top. Then he looked at the clock on the wall, shut the classroom door, and returned to the desk. "OK, people, detention has officially begun. Phones on the desk now." He thumped his pointer finger on Mrs. Howard's desktop.

Cecil and Colin grumbled as they pulled out their phones and deposited them on the corner of the desk. The bigger inconvenience for them seemed to be the walk from the table to Mrs. Howard's desk and back to the table again. Clark offered to take mine up for me. Despite losing my phone privileges at home, my parents allowed me to keep it during the day in case of emergencies; a by-product of living in a school-shooting world. I handed it to him.

Mr. Fischetti called out the roster of the damned and singled me out. "I'm surprised to see you here, Wylie."

I wanted to crawl under the table. It was bad enough being the only girl, but I was going to have to face him tomorrow and the rest of the school year.

"She pleads innocent, Mr. Fish," said Clark.

"You're her attorney of record?"

He nodded. "*Pro bono.* My client has suffered a miscarriage of justice."

"Too late. She's doing time like the rest of us. OK…" He cleared his throat and spoke with a teacherly voice: "We're all stuck here for two hours. No talking and no sleeping. You can do homework or write your name a thousand times, for all I care. Graffiti the desks and I'll make you lick them clean." *Pretty funny, considering all we art students ever did was draw and paint on them.* "If you have a question, raise your hand. If you have to use the bathroom, speak now or forever hold your…you get the idea."

No one said anything.

"Anderson," called Mr. Fischetti.

Clark sat up at attention in his seat. "Sir!"

He motioned Clark to the front of the room, divided the stack of papers in half, and handed them to him, along with a red pen. "Correct these. Answer key's on top. Don't put a grade on them; just the number incorrect."

"Sure thing," said Clark.

"If you try to fudge the results of someone you know, I'm going to make you serve out the rest of detention in your gym locker, got it?"

Clark caught me stifling a giggle, and then saluted. "Yes, sir."

He instructed Clark to sit at the table closest to the door, and then commanded me to join him. I don't know why, other than he wanted to keep an eye on us. Although if I was such a model student, what did he think I was going to do in the back of the room, run some kind of hall-pass forgery racket? I lugged my backpack, purse, and jacket with me. Felt weird to be sitting in what was normally Kelly Poindexter's seat.

I glanced at the wall clock. Two thirty. Ugh. It was going to be the longest two hours of my life. I raised my hand, and Mr. Fischetti acknowledged me.

"Would it be OK for me to work on my painting?" I asked, pointing to the easels in the back.

He considered the request, and then turned it down. "Why should you get to have all the fun?"

Normally Mr. Fish was cool, but *come on...* So much for doing whatever we wanted.

"Can't blame a girl for trying," I heard Clark mutter under his breath. I looked at him and we exchanged glances, seeming to understand each other perfectly, translated into something like this:

Me: *I know, right? Like, painting is work.*

Clark: *He's taking out on you the fact that he got stuck here with the rest of us. Don't sweat it.*

Instead I opened my folder and took out the "Letter from Birmingham Jail" that Andi sent me the other night. Prior to coming to detention, I'd stopped in the library and used the computer to download and print it out on the off-chance that I wouldn't be allowed to draw or paint. I don't know why I'd bothered, other than I figured it would kill time. I still didn't understand why Andi had sent it to me in the first place other than to either punish or torture me. Why couldn't she and I have made a date for retail therapy instead? I mean, sure, it sucked that Christina's been trash-talking me, and so far, to my knowledge, no one had come to my defense, but that's not exactly the same thing as segregation and a hundred years of oppression.

It was either that or homework, and I wasn't in the mood to do homework.

I took out my drafting pencil and began to read, trying to shut out the rest of the world by leaning on my elbows and using my hands like blinders on each side of my head. Andi had taught me that when reading something complex, do a straightforward read-through the first time and, with a pencil, make a check mark next to sections I understood and question marks next to sections I didn't. For the second read-through, I was supposed to go more slowly, making notes to summarize each paragraph, circle words whose meanings I didn't know, and ask specific questions for parts I didn't understand. "Talk to the text," Andi had said. "Pretend you're having a conversation about it with the writer." At first I'd had no clue that she'd meant "text" as the thing you were reading rather than what you send back and forth with your friends on your phone. I wondered if all college students referred to their assigned readings this way.

It's not that the individual words were hard to read. But overall, I didn't understand what Martin Luther King was trying to explain. Andi had also taught me to identify "audience" and "context" right away, such as the year something was written, who it was written for, where it was originally published, and what was happening in the world at the time. So I'd started there and made notes at the top of the first page:

Audience: *Six clergymen in Birmingham, Alabama*
Context: *Civil rights movement. 1963. Martin Luther King is in jail*

in Birmingham, Alabama, because he marched without a permit. His audience doesn't seem to be receptive. (It wasn't published?)
Objective: Martin Luther King is writing a response to the clergymen. ????????

It turned out there were two letters. The first was short, from the clergymen to a newspaper. The second was from Martin Luther King to the clergymen and way longer. It took me an hour just to read the first two pages of the document, and I'd littered the margins and every bit of white space with question marks, requests for further clarification or explanation, and circled words.

I nearly jumped out of my seat when I heard a voice say from behind my shoulder, " 'Letter from Birmingham Jail'... What class is *this* reading for?"

I'd been so engrossed that I hadn't seen or heard Mr. Fischetti get up from behind his desk to presumably stretch his legs and eavesdrop on what we were all doing.

For some reason I felt the need to cover up the papers, although he'd obviously already gotten an eyeful. "Oh, it's—it's not for a class," I stammered. "It's, um... it's something a college professor gave me. She tutors me for English—now you know why my grade picked up so much from last year—and she told me to read this."

He physically moved my hands away and picked up the pages—why did teachers think they had the right to do such things?—and proceeded to scan them as I helplessly watched. "This is some very sophisticated note-taking, Wylie."

"Really?" I said. Felt like all I was doing was flaunting my stupidity.

"Also explains why you're doing so well on the literature tests."

"Thank you." In my peripheral vision I spotted Clark Anderson's glistening eyes—God, they were like little sunbeams shooting though his lenses. My heart fluttered. Then he gave me a thumbs-up.

I diverted my attention again, wishing for an off switch for blushing.

Mr. Fischetti looked at me. "Will you write me an essay about what you learn from this reading? I'll give you extra credit."

Extra credit? Seriously?

"I guess so," I said. "If I have time."

"I'll give you until the end of the term."

"OK," I said. Two months seemed doable.

He moved on to Clark. "You finished, Anderson?"

Clark sat up at attention again. "Yes, sir. Almost." Funny how some students could be so nonchalant, mocking, even, of a teacher and that teacher took it in stride, while other students could attempt the same thing and the same teacher would admonish them for being disrespectful. Mr. Fischetti was used to kids calling him "Mr. Fish," and although I called him that outside of class, I never said it to his face. But Clark's overall demeanor with him made me envious. I'll bet he was like that with every teacher, even the nasty subs. And I'll bet even the nastiest of the nasty subs adored him to pieces.

After Mr. Fischetti returned my pages to me, I put them back in my folder (my brain ached) and took out my sketchbook instead—not the new one Roxanne gave me for my birthday, but one I always carried in my backpack. He said I wasn't allowed to paint, but mentioned nothing about drawing. At first I sketched Colin sleeping sitting up, until he was jolted awake by Cecil picking up a textbook and letting it crash to the desk. Cruel. Then I sketched the stack of Clark's books, his car keys perched slipshod on top of them. When he spied what I was up to, he leaned over to get a better look and said in a soft voice, "That's really good."

I nodded so as not to speak.

"Which one is yours?" he asked, nudging his head in the direction of the paintings in the back.

What, was he trying to get me in trouble? I tried to inconspicuously point it out.

"The red one with the weird-looking snake?" he asked.

I shook my head and pointed to the right of it. He shrugged. Finally, I whispered, "The still life. Pile of shoes."

"Ohhhhh." He tilted his head to the side and inspected my painting as if he were trying to make sense of it. "It's good. I like it. You're a good artist, Wylie Baker. Is that what you're going to go to college for?"

Good question.

"I don't know yet," I said. "What are you going for?"

"I don't know yet either. I was accepted to Edmund College, but I have no clue what to major in. I like the humanities, but good luck getting a job."

"That name rings a bell," I said.

"Edmund College? It's in Massachusetts. Near Amherst."

And then it hit me: I'd once seen Andi wearing a sweatshirt from Edmund College that had belonged to her husband Sam, the one who died. He used to teach there.

"Ohmigod, I know people who live there!" I blurted.

"Wylie, don't make me give you another day of detention. Anderson, quit getting her in trouble," said Mr. Fischetti.

"But we're talking about college and advancing our education," said Clark.

"We've got less than fifteen minutes left—can we please finish it out in peace?" he pleaded.

"So what would happen if you let us out fifteen minutes early?" asked Clark, not even trying to keep his voice down.

Mr. Fischetti gave him a *give it up* look.

"Seriously, who's around to find out?"

"Anderson, your senioritis is at an all-time feverish high. Take a pill."

"Really, man, shut the fuck up," I heard Colin mutter.

"Hey," Mr. Fischetti warned Colin.

"I wouldn't tell anyone," said Clark. I had to cover my mouth to keep from laughing, which I knew would egg him on. And it did. "Wylie won't tell anyone either. Right, Wylie?" he said to me.

"Keep me out of this," I said.

"Smart girl," said Mr. Fish. "Anderson: What Jamison said."

"I'm Furman," said Colin.

"Sorry," said Mr. Fish. "What Furman said."

"Two minutes have passed already. Conversation passes the time. Why torture yourself by sitting in silence and instead get to know us a little better?" said Clark.

Mr. Fischetti looked exasperated, as if Clark had finally worn him down. He looked at the clock on the art room wall, and then at his watch.

"Hey look, that clock over there is ten minutes slow. Time to go, everyone." And he gave everyone a *this stays between us* look. Colin and Cecil instantly came to life, collected their phones, and went on their way. Clark sincerely thanked him.

"You're a piece of work, Anderson. Thank god you're going to be someone else's problem next year. Where'd you say you were going? Edmund University?"

"Edmund College," Clark corrected.

"It's in Massachusetts," I filled in. "In the same area as Smith and Northampton U and UMass Amherst," I said. "I spend time up there once in awhile. It's a nice area."

"Good, then you can come visit me," said Clark, and he grinned again. I smiled and blushed again.

Mr. Fischetti handed us our phones. "Wylie, I meant what I said about that essay. I hope you'll do it."

"OK," I said. "Thanks for the opportunity."

I was about to speed-dial my mom to ask her to pick me up when Clark caught me off guard by asking me if I wanted a ride.

"Oh," I said. "Um, sure. OK. Thanks."

Ever since I snuck away to meet my biological father for the first time last fall, and even though I swore I hadn't hitchhiked, my mother has been adamant in knowing whom, if someone other than Trish, was giving me a ride. I should have called her. But I didn't want Clark to think I was some kind of baby. Besides, *Ohmigod!*

"No problem. You need to go to your locker or anything?"

"I'm good."

"Cool," he said. "Let's go."

Chapter Six

The April sun still shone brightly for late afternoon as I crossed the asphalt wasteland with Clark Anderson to his car, realizing for the first time how tall and gangly he was. "So that wasn't so bad, was it?" he said.

I shrugged and looked behind me, the ancient brick building shrinking from our sight with every footstep. "Could've been worse." I paused before asking, "How many more do you have?"

"Another week after this one. I have a detention hour for every class I cut. Already put in two weeks, two hours per detention."

Holy crapdoodle!

"Did you only cut Study Hall?"

"Usually. That, and Phys Ed. And a couple of AP classes."

"Why'd you cut in the first place?"

"Because I have more important things to do than sit in a stuffy room and fall asleep from boredom that makes you die inside."

"You could do homework," I suggested.

"I'm a *senior*," he said, as if I should know better. Then he nudged my arm with the back of his hand, and it was as if he'd sent off a chain reaction of falling dominos through my circulatory system. Dominos on fire.

"Maybe I'll start coming again just to see you," he said.

Ohmigod, was that a flirty thing or a friendly thing? Who cares? Yes, please!

I didn't answer him. We arrived at his car, an olive green Volkswagen Jetta. "Meet Oliver," he said.

"You named your car?"

"Sure, why not? It's a hand-me-down," he said apologetically. "Don't get me wrong, I'm not complaining; a ride's a ride. But I'm saving for my dream car: a 1968 Pontiac GTO, fully loaded and restored. There's a collector who will sell me one if I can cough up the cash. It needs a lot of work, but that will be the fun part. I'm about three quarters there with savings. But Edmund College doesn't have campus housing so I'm going to have to find a place to live, and there goes my moolah."

"Your parents can't help with that?" I asked. "Or student loans or something?"

"They're doing what they can. But I want to pay for as much of my education as I can on my own. Makes it more mine that way." He started the engine, and a clamor of guitars and cymbals bombarded my eardrums. He quickly turned down the volume. "Sorry about that. What do you like?"

"Do you know The Cure? I've been listening to them a lot lately. Them and The Smiths. And a lot of British pop from the early eighties."

"I'm not surprised, based on your party. I might have The Smiths somewhere. Where do you live?"

I gawked at him for a second until my brain caught up. "Oh. I'm here in West Hartford."

He chuckled. "I need your address, silly."

I laughed to cover up my mortification and told him my address. He entered it into the GPS app on his phone. Probably thought I was some kind of idiot and was better off relying on his GPS than asking me for directions. He spun the tires and screeched out of the parking lot. Oh geez. Maybe my mother was right about my calling her. I wouldn't want to explain how I got into the car of a strange senior and wound up in a ditch. I was planning to get my permit and take Driver's Ed over the summer, but if she found out what I was doing right now, I'd be lucky to be allowed to ride my bicycle.

"I have to go straight home," I said, feeling like a middle-schooler. "Still grounded."

"No worries," he said.

"I get paroled tomorrow."

"Cool."

My phone pinged. Text message from Bottsy. I ignored it and frantically searched my brain for a conversation starter. "So I'm guessing you don't know many sophs," I said as he browsed through the satellite radio channels for mutually enjoyable music. *Wow. Brilliant. You came up with that all by yourself?*

"I don't go out of my way to avoid them, but we don't cross paths much," he said. "Why?"

"I don't know." Ohmigod, I was making such a fool of myself.

"You're cool, Wylie. I mean, I've only known you for two hours, but it feels longer, doesn't it?"

"That's because detention was woefully long."

He laughed, although not at me personally. Made me feel less moronic. "Good point. But still. From day one I could tell you're cool. And you're good at drawing too."

Day one!

"Do you do anything creative?" I asked.

"I play keyboards a little bit. Used to be in a band too, but they had delusions of grandeur—recording deals and world tours and *American Idol*. Not for me." He turned onto the main road and headed for the heart of town that seemed to be collectively getting out of work and school and extra-curricular activities.

"So whom do you know up in Massachusetts?" he asked.

"My biological dad lives there."

Wow. Did I really just say that out loud?

"You're adopted?" he asked.

"Not really," I said. "But I'd appreciate it if you didn't mention it to anyone. In fact, I can't believe I just told a total stranger that."

"Hey, we spent an entire detention together. In some cultures that makes us married." I couldn't help but laugh, despite my trying not to giggle like a little girl at everything he said. "Seriously, no worries," he said. "What's said in Oliver stays in Oliver."

"Thanks," I said. "It's kind of a weird situation. I didn't meet him until recently. He never even knew about me."

"Is he a jerk or something?" asked Clark.

"Oh, no, he's massively cool. But he's also massively protective about his identity—not that he's ashamed of me or anything like that," I quickly added. "In fact, I think sometimes he wants to shout it from the rooftops. He's sorry he missed out."

"Your mom never told him?"

"Like I said, it's a weird situation."

He held up his hands like I was putting a gun to his head, "Hey, I don't mean to pry."

"No, it's OK," I said. "But it's weird telling someone I just met." And yet, I wanted to keep talking about it with him.

"Sometimes it's a lot easier to tell a stranger your deepest secrets than the people closest to you. It's why people love bartenders and hairstylists."

I suddenly felt like I could tell Clark Anderson anything.

"You know, I'm thinking of becoming a hairstylist. Got any secrets you want to spill?" I said as a joke. Clark started straight ahead at the road, his mischievous grin implying he had plenty of secrets.

"Not right now, thanks," he said. "Maybe because I know you too well." He winked at me.

Oh my God. I like Clark Anderson. Like, LIKE like.

When was the last time I'd liked a guy before? Had I ever? And I'm not talking about celebrity crushes, but a real guy in the flesh. I love Bottsy—always have—but I'd never seen him as anything more than a friend or a brother. Two years ago we kissed for the first time at a party. But it was weird and we vowed never to do it again. Not that he was bad-looking—he carried a slight pudge, wore his strawberry-blond hair short, almost buzzed, and had a fondness for polo shirts and khakis. He'd taken an etiquette class once and from then on opened doors or pulled chairs out for girls, myself included, and even though he wasn't popular, no one really bullied him either. More like he blended into the background. Maybe too much.

But he was always there for me, and if he, Roxanne, and I weren't hanging out together or Roxanne was busy, I could always call him if he wasn't working his part-time job at the Stop N Shop. Going a day without talking to Bottsy was like going a day without food and water. Ditto for Roxanne.

"You know, he was at my party," I said. "My biological dad, I mean."

"Oh yeah? Which one was he?"

"The Simon LeBon guy with the tie tucked in his shirt."

"Rings a bell," said Clark.

"You like working for my uncle?" I asked.

He shrugged. "He's nice. I mean, it's just a job, you know?"

I nodded. "I guess."

Clark and I continued to talk as the GPS directed him to turn left, then right, then another left. We cruised through my neighborhood, and I couldn't help but notice how all the houses looked alike, one split-level after another in various earthy colors of vinyl siding and black shutters sandwiched between a dropcloth of grassy lawns and a ceiling of clear sky and cotton clouds. It all looked so matchy-matchy. In no time he pulled up to my house (the split-levels ended and the colonials began), and I was secretly begging for another five minutes. I was tempted to tell him his GPS was wrong and have him drop me off somewhere else just so I could talk to him a little bit longer.

"Thanks for the ride," I said.

"Thanks for making detention more bearable," he said.

I couldn't even look at him, lest I start grinning like a goofball.

"You should keep coming back to Study Hall," I said.

"Well, I kind of have to. But I will definitely show up if you bring your sketchbook."

"Deal," I said.

"In that case, I'll see you tomorrow. But first, give me your phone." I passed it to him. He entered his number into it, and handed it back to me. "Feel free to text me."

"Thanks," I said. My hand shook so much I thought I might drop the phone. "Don't you want my number?"

"I'll get it when you text me."

He spun the tires and screeched away again as I entered my house and bounded straight upstairs to my room, closing and locking my door and blasting Simple Minds' "Don't You Forget About Me" (how could I not?). I took out my new sketchbook and a charcoal pencil and quickly committed Clark Anderson's features to the page: the tousled hair, dappled irises, dark, rounded eyebrows, small chin.

And then it hit me: *I'm still grounded!* I wasn't allowed to text anyone the minute I got home from school. My parents would be checking. I had gotten away using Trish's phone with Andi, but I wasn't about to tempt fate twice.

I couldn't even text him to tell him why I wouldn't be texting him. Ughhhhhh!

Now what?

Chapter Seven

I couldn't remember the last time I was excited to go to school, and I agonized over what to wear. I wanted to be neither too casual nor obviously trying too hard. Plus there was no guarantee that Clark was actually going to show up to Study Hall, which, for me, was the third-to-last class of the day.

Normally I sought Trish's advice on things like this. She knew how to accessorize and put an outfit together, whereas I was better at selecting and applying makeup, and picking out the correct hair products and tools and using them. It was a winning combination; we had fun when we collaborated. Sometimes I forgot Trish was my stepsister and not my biological sister. She seemed to as well, although I was too young too remember how she'd had difficulty adjusting to me when our parents had gotten married, was fiercely jealous of my mom and me. At least that's what my mom had told me one night following a massive fight they'd gotten into. In recent years, she related to my mom in ways that were respectful, but not necessarily affectionate. I don't know why she was different with me. She'd once told me that she'd always wanted a sister. I guess in the end, I was as good as any.

I hadn't yet told her about Clark, however—not only because she'd been at work last night, but also because chances were good that she already knew him, was even in a few classes with him. Funny how I didn't even think to ask Clark if he knew her, or that my last name didn't ring any bells for him. I was used to teachers asking me if I was Patricia Baker's sister on the first day of class, standing in her academic shadow. Usually it didn't bother me. Our parents never set us up for competition, and we gave each other social space in school. Like me, Trish was the type of person who was accepted by every clique but joined none and still had plenty of friends. But I was afraid that somehow my letting Trish in on this would mean she'd somehow become Clark's friend too, if she wasn't already, and take him away from me.

An impatient Trish left without me (she usually drove us to and from school), and my mother warned me not to miss the bus or I'd be walking to school. I settled on skinny jeans, plum-colored tee with cami-sleeves, a cropped, short-sleeved black denim jacket, and canary yellow flats. I brushed out my hair past my shoulders—next week I was planning to dye it from black to a warm, caramel color— and went for a more natural spring look makeup-wise, copying from a magazine ad taped to my mirror. My nails were in desperate need of a manicure, jagged free edges with flecks of paint stuck underneath. Hopefully Clark wouldn't notice, or hadn't already noticed.

I wound up running for the bus and barely catching it.

Every class was an exercise in fidgeting, with seconds slowed to minutes and hours slowed to epochs.

"Geez, Wylie, what is wrong with you today?" Roxanne asked me at lunch. "You look like you're about to jump out of your skin."

"Your outfit is nice, though," said Bottsy. "You look pretty."

Did Roxanne just huff under her breath?

"Thanks," I said. "Is it too much?"

"For what?" asked Roxanne. "Do you have a date after school or something?"

I was just about to take the plunge and tell them when Bottsy said, "Of course not. She dressed up just for me," and he put his arm around me.

I pulled his arm off and replied, "Yeah, right."

I caught the look—first in his eyes, then in hers. Bottsy, wounded, like I'd just kicked him. Roxanne, glowering, like she was about to kick me.

"I'm sorry, Botts. I'm just...I—"

"No worries," said Bottsy.

Before I could get out another word, Roxanne stood up and flung her backpack over her shoulder. "You are so dense sometimes," she said to me. "And *you*," she said to Bottsy, "need to wake up." With that she picked up the remains of her lunch and stormed off.

I looked at Bottsy in utter bewilderment. "*What* is *her* problem?"

Bottsy fixed his focus on his sandwich. "It's nothing," he said, his tone matching his wounded eyes, before extracting a crumpled piece of paper jammed into his math textbook. "I've got to finish last night's homework before the bell rings," he said, and ignored me for the rest of the lunch period. Only thing that would've made things worse was if Christina had shown up. Luckily she was back to skipping lunch, so I was able to avoid her, although Caitlyn reported that Christina bragged about my getting detention. HA! Joke was on her. Had she been there she totally would've tried to get Clark's attention and probably would've succeeded too. Christina was good at getting guys' attention, not to mention getting people to do what she wanted. She and Hillary had started a campaign whereas whenever one of their minions passed me in the hall or sat near me in class, they'd loudly whisper *Loser* to me. Please. Be original.

That said, four hours in and it was starting to grate on me.

Finally, Study Hall.

What little of the panini sandwich I'd tried to eat during lunch churned mercilessly as I entered the room. Study Hall was the one class where we didn't have assigned seating, but we'd all been sitting in the same seats since the first day. The room was twice as big as most classrooms and used as a practice room for the orchestra. Twice as many students too. We also didn't have much by way of discipline, other than that we were supposed to be quiet and not leave our seats without permission.

Not much different than detention, come to think of it. Although we were allowed to work or study in groups and talk quietly, though.

I looked around and tried to picture where Clark normally sat—it must've been in back, because I still couldn't remember seeing him. I focused on the doorway, my anxiety increasing as practically the entire student body except Clark Anderson meandered in and filled the surrounding seats.

He's not coming.

And then, just as the bell rang, my churning stomach turned into fluttering butterflies when I caught the glint of the zippers on his biker jacket. He didn't even scan the room to look for me. Spotted me instantly and motioned to the back of the room and two unoccupied desks next to each other. It felt weird to stand up and move—like I was somehow disrupting the earth's equilibrium, and like everyone was watching us even though no one gave a crap.

Clark was dressed almost exactly the same as yesterday—jeans, a Punk Masters graphic T-shirt, and leather jacket. His hair looked like he'd recently run a comb through it.

"Wylie Baker," he said as if to refresh his memory. "You never texted me."

Ohmigod, he actually *wanted* me to text him! He *waited*! And I totally let him down. I *am* a loser.

"Oh, I totally forgot that I was still grounded and without phone privileges," I said. "Sorry."

He smiled. "No worries. And you did mention you were grounded. I should've remembered. You bring your sketchbook?"

I unzipped my backpack and pulled it out. "I always have it with me."

He feigned disappointment. "And here I thought I was special."

"Sorry," I said again. No, not loser. *Moron.*

"Kidding, Wylie."

I blushed. "Guess I'll learn humor when I'm a junior," I said.

He laughed. "You already did," he said, and began to flip through my sketchbook, complimenting me and asking questions about when I'd started drawing, my favorite painting techniques, and if I'd ever sold any of my work. We talked in hushed tones, and I almost forgot the room was full of people. Clark seemed oblivious to it as well, albeit in different ways. More like he just didn't care—about the rules, about the hierarchy of monitors and teachers and administrators. I kind of admired and even envied his ability to be so blasé about it.

"So can you do a drawing right now, on the spot?"

"Of what?" I asked.

"I don't know…" He looked around. "Wow, there's even less inspiration here than in detention. God, this place is so depressing."

I concurred. "You have no idea how lucky you are to be graduating this year. I'm stuck in this prison for two more years. My parents won't even consider the idea of me going to another school."

"Even your real dad?" he said. I sent him a nonverbal message: *Ix-nay on the iological-bay ad-day.* He received it, comprehended, and changed the subject. "Hey, can you draw a self-portrait?"

"Not right this second. I'd have to look in a mirror or copy a photograph. Even then the last time I tried it came out craptastic."

"How about me? Could you draw me if I sat here and posed for you?"

My heart was beating so loud and fast I thought it was going to grow legs, jump out of my chest, and run away. "That would be pretty boring for you, wouldn't it? Not to mention that posing is harder than it seems. After awhile your muscles get tired."

"You've posed?"

"We all had to take turns for the figure-drawing unit in Drawing and Painting last quarter."

"Clothed, I assume," he said, and grinned devilishly. I could've died right on the spot. "Seriously, Wylie, you can draw me right now if you want."

Drawing you was not what I had in mind...

"I guess," I said. "I don't know, I'd be kind of nervous. Too afraid I'll mess it up."

"OK, so we'll save it for when you get up the nerve. But I do want a Wylie Baker Original at some point."

"Sure," I said. "Then when I'm famous you'll sell it for millions."

He caught and held my gaze for what felt like eternity, and said earnestly, "Don't be too sure of that."

Oh. My God. I am a pool of melted butter.

Clark continued to interview me with questions about my favorite bands ("Not really, I just like a bunch of different random songs"), movies ("Everything has too much CGI"), and books ("I don't read too much, but Andi got me a Kindle Paperwhite for my birthday. I haven't used it yet"—he laughed when I called it a "typical English teacher gift.").

"Ask me about my favorite artists," I said. "I'll talk your ear off. So he did, and I told him how much I loved Monet and Manet and Van Gogh and Dali, and that David loved those same artists, and how bad my first attempt at Impressionist painting came out, and why knowing how to draw in perspective comes in handy when you're doing a haircut. He seemed genuinely interested in everything I had to say, yet shared very little in return. He was obviously a reader and a movie and music buff, and I was shamefully, pathetically not; but he promised to make a list of books for me to read.

The bell rang. Never had I been so disappointed for Study Hall to end, nor had I ever been so awake without consuming a drop of Red Bull.

"Where do you go from here?" I asked.

"AP History," he replied. "You?"

"Science."

"McNally?" he asked.

I shook my head. "I wish. Webber."

He made a barfing gesture. "Tell me about it," I said.

"Well, have fun. Detention is going to suck without you there. You sure you don't want to join me? Pull a fire alarm? Graffiti the bathroom? Shoot spitballs at Webber?"

I shook my head emphatically. "No way. I'm on the straight and narrow."

He gently elbowed me in the ribs. "Can't blame a guy for trying."

"Not that I'm encouraging this, but just curious—what happens if you blow off any of your classes now?"

"I don't graduate," he replied.

"Well, in that case, get going to AP History, young man," I said in a mock teacher voice.

He stood at attention and saluted me the way he'd done Mr. Fischetti in detention the day before. "Yes, ma'am." We reached the end of the hallway and I was about to turn the corner when he said, "I'm in the other direction. Same Bat-time, same Bat-channel tomorrow?"

I looked at him quizzically as students hurried past us. He looked back at me, shocked. "Don't tell me you don't know what that's from! Ohhh, Wylie Baker, you disappoint me."

I knew he was kidding, but I felt like a total failure.

"Well, now you've got extra homework," he said as the final bell rang. "See ya." And with that he ran off.

I have no memory of my classes after that.

The minute I got home from school I Googled the phrase *Same Bat-time, Same Bat-channel*, and could hardly wait to send Clark my first text, although I knew I'd have to at least wait until his detention was over.

I also Googled *Clark Anderson*. An array of Facebook photos popped up, with him playing keyboards, his hair longer (I liked it the way it was now) his eyes squeezed tightly shut when he sang. He wore the biker jacket in almost every photo. There were also tagged photos of him at parties with his arms around girls I didn't recognize, probably all juniors and seniors and perhaps even a few who already graduated. I also saw that he was on the honor roll here at Ford, and there was even a YouTube video of him doing a duet piano recital with someone named Lulu Lawrence. However, when I clicked on it, a message came up saying the content had been blocked.

Next, I clicked on his Facebook page and deliberated on whether to send him a friend request. I wasn't on much lately, especially since Christina's "loser" campaign had crossed over to Facebook with her minions tagging me. I deactivated Notifications.

That evening at dinner, I piped up. "Hey Mom, did you watch the TV show *Batman* when you were a kid?"

"Your father did," she said, nodding in Dad's direction. Lately it had been weirding me out that David's image was coming to mind at the exact same time every time she used the word *father* instead of *dad*. "I thought it was stupid."

"It was campy," said Dad. "I loved it."

"What's 'campy'?" I asked.

"Something that doesn't take itself too seriously. Kind of like deliberately cheesy," said Dad.

"You just watched because you had a crush on Catwoman," said Mom.

"Who didn't?" said Dad, and laughed. "Why do you ask, Wylie?"

"No reason," I said, and took an abnormal interest in the roasted potatoes on my plate in an attempt to ignore Trish's curious stare boring a hole into me.

I had somehow managed to hold off texting Clark until after dinner.

Batman TV series from the 60s.

Two minutes later my phone pinged.

Gold star for you. Watch it. Learn it. Recite it.

A second text followed: *If you ever use u for you, r for are, OMG, LOL, and all those other annoying abbreviations, then you are dead to me.*

I giggled and texted back: *U r full of it. ;)*

One more message: *Well played, Wylie Baker. See you tomorrow?*

I typed carefully: *Same Bat-time, same Bat-channel, Clark Anderson.*

In between watching clips of *Batman* on YouTube—the guy who played him had, like, no decent body whatsoever, and the other one who played Robin was obsessed with the word "golly"—I must have checked my phone a gazillion times for a new text from Clark, or to re-read our text exchange, sporadically texting with Bottsy in the meantime. Roxanne still hadn't spoken to me since lunch, and Bottsy's explanation was that she bombed Ms. Galluppi's pop quiz. Seemed like an overreaction to me.

I finally went to bed. A whirlwind of elation mixed with confusion swirled within me, from head to toe, like a funnel cloud. Should I read into his not wanting to continue our text chat? Or should I just be glad he texted me at all? Or should I not have been the first one to text him? Trish says when you make the first move you give a guy all the power.

Maybe it was time for me to talk to someone about this.

Chapter Eight

The next day in Study Hall I found out why Clark didn't text with me. He handed me a piece of spiral notebook paper folded in quarters.

"I wrote you a letter to pass the time in detention yesterday. Didn't want to chat with you last night and make it obsolete. Do me a favor: read it now and reply so I'll have something to do at today's detention."

"You're going to sit here and watch me read your letter and then write one back to you?"

"I'll keep myself occupied, promise." He pulled out a tattered book and showed it to me before opening it to a dog-eared page. It was called *The Hitchhiker's Guide to the Galaxy*.

I un-quartered the notebook paper, smoothed it out, and began to read the scrawl of handwriting that was characteristic of so many boys I knew.

> *Dear Wylie,*
>
> *Since you're not here for me to bother I decided to pass the time in detention by writing to you. The art of letter-writing is dead, and I think you and I should single-handedly revive it. Sometimes I think I was born in the wrong decade. Have you ever felt that way?*

Mr. Fish is stuck with us for another day—Cecil and that other dude are back, as well as two freshmen I've never seen before. Looking at them makes me wonder if I was that short and scrawny when I was a freshman.

A chortle escaped me, and I covered my mouth in self-consciousness after the fact. But when I looked up at Clark, he seemed engrossed in his book, although I caught him darting his eyes at me for a second.

I came to the art room a little early to check out your painting. I'll say it again: you're really good, and I think you should go to college to become a graphic designer. At least that way you won't be a starving artist (although I have no clue what graphic artists make).

Can I just tell you how sick I am of this art room and this institution and this waste of time and life called high school and adolescence? I am so ready to get out into the world, although a sleepy little place like Edmund College isn't exactly the high life. What can I say? At least it's someplace I can live on my own and enjoy the scenery, and I can still root for the Red Sox. Which reminds me, have we talked sports teams yet? We root for the Red Sox, the Patriots, the Celtics, and I guess the Bruins by default, but who cares about hockey? Did you see what I did there, Baker? I wrote WE. As in, you are dead to me if you like the Yankees or the Mets (but especially the Yankees), the Jets or the Giants, the Lakers, and hockey in general. We won't even discuss college sports given that I'm going somewhere that probably doesn't even have a Division III chess club.

If you haven't been able to tell yet, I'm originally from

Massachusetts. Framingham, to be exact. My parents moved here when I was about ten, then they got divorced two years later. Shitty, huh? I never did quite acclimate to Connecticut.

I feel pressure to get all philosophical on you and talk about God and religion or whatever. But the thing is, I really don't give a shit about God or philosophy. Don't get me wrong, I'm not exactly an atheist, and I'm not a massive partier (and you don't seem to be either, which is good), and don't hate me for saying something so clichéd and stupid, but I really do get high on life. I think there is good in the world if you look hard enough for it and don't go acting like an asshole yourself. And I can tell just by the little interaction we've had that you're a good egg, Wylie Baker. (Where does that expression come from, anyway? Why call someone an egg? Why not tell someone they're a good kiwi instead?)

Wylie, may I ask if you've ever had a boyfriend? I had a girlfriend. She was my age, but graduated a year ahead of me. (She's wicked smart.) We broke up around September last year. (What was going on in your life last September?) She didn't want a long-distance relationship, and she didn't want any more ties to high school. I can understand that, I guess, and I kind of saw the signs that she was losing interest, but it still bummed me out. I always knew I was more serious about her than she was about me, and I have a feeling she wasn't intellectually stimulated by me, but I can't help that. I'm not stupid by any means, but I'm no genius either. And if I take one more standardized test I'm going to set fire to Scantron sheets and Number Two pencils everywhere. But I digress.

I hope I didn't get too personal with you. You're not

moonlighting as a bartender by any chance, are you?

There's a lot of time left in detention, but I can't think of anything else to write. At least I just now used up ten minutes staring at this piece of paper trying to think of something clever. Besides, I think Mr. Fish wants me to correct papers again. You couldn't pay me enough to be a teacher. But hey, he's cool for the most part so I'll do the slave labor for him.

I hope you're doing something fun right now.

Your friend,

Clark

P.S. Do you think Clark is a nerdy name? I've always liked it, but lately I've been thinking I should change it to something more distinguished, like Harrison. Have I mentioned how cool the name Wylie is? Yes, yes I have. What's that you say? Shut up now? Ok.

Wow.

Holy moly, who was this guy? Not a genius? Could have fooled me. I'd never read a letter like this before. Come to think of it, I don't think I'd ever read a letter, period. And most guys I knew spoke in one-syllable words. They certainly didn't use words like "acclimate" and "digress." My guess was that the average teenage male also didn't write like this either.

And what about that whole thing about him having had a serious girlfriend? Which of those girls he had his arm around in those photos was her? They probably had sex. Lots of it.

Wylie Baker, you are out of your league.

Clark Anderson was *a writer.* And he wanted me to write back to him? I was totally screwed.

Not to mention the actual thud of my heart when I saw the words *Your friend*. Well, at least I knew where we stood.

I re-folded the paper and put it in the secret compartment of my purse. Then I looked up at him. He seemed less engrossed in his book than before.

"So, you really want me to write you back now? Seems kind of silly to do that when you and I could talk instead," I said.

"Didn't you see what I wrote?" he said. "I want us to revive the art of letter-writing. Seriously."

I suddenly wondered if Clark Anderson had somehow time-traveled from the past and was now stuck here, trying to make the best of it. Or maybe he was a non-sparkly vampire who was more mature than everyone else his age because he'd lived here for like six thousand years.

"If you and I are only writing letters to each other, then how will anyone else know about it, and know to revive it?" I asked.

"Well, I guess that's the thing. We have to start writing letters to other people as well."

"Too much work," I said. He laughed.

Making Clark Anderson laugh was quickly moving up the list of things that made me feel warm and gooey inside. I just wished it wasn't when I was being totally serious.

"So come on, get going. There's not much time left in Study Hall."

"I can't just write a letter on demand, Clark. Especially if I know you're watching me do it."

"Who's watching? I'm sitting here reading my book."

"Still, you know I'm doing it. You might as well be looking over my shoulder."

He sighed demonstratively. "OK, Wylie Baker. For you I'll make an exception. But if we're going to sit here and talk to each other now, then everything in the letter is off-limits."

"Deal," I said. He closed his book and rested it on the desk, and we looked at each other for a moment. I couldn't think of a single thing to say, and apparently the same thing happened to him because we both sat there in awkward silence, looking at each other blankly. Upon recognition, we both burst into stifled laughter.

"Well, so much for that idea," said Clark.

"Maybe I'd better do homework or something," I said.

He looked at the clock. "We've got ten minutes left. How about you draw me instead."

Gosh, he was pushy. "In ten minutes?" I said. "I don't think so."

"Do one of those quick sketches."

"Like a gesture drawing?" I said. "I guess so." I took out my sketchbook and opened it to one of the few remaining clean pages. Then I extracted a pencil and inspected it, frowning. "This point is dull."

"You don't carry a sharpener around with you?"

I shook my head. "David—*my biological dad*," I mouthed, "showed me how to sharpen pencils with an X-Acto knife. Now that's the only way I like my pencils sharpened. And since they don't let us carry X-Acto knives in school…"

"Well, do the best you can," he said.

I'd done sixty-second sketches as part of Drawing and Painting class, so it's not like I couldn't do it, but trying to sketch with a dull-pointed pencil and a shaky hand due to the fact that *ohmigod the guy I like wants me to draw him!* was like trying to sketch blindfolded with your dominant hand tied behind your back. In fact, I probably could've done a better sketch under those conditions. "Look over there," I instructed, pointing to a spot in the room that would give him a three-quarter pose. He obeyed with a "Yes, ma'am."

I moved the pencil rapidly in one continuous line, alternating my focus between the page and Clark, hyper-aware that I was focused so intensely on him and secretly praying I wouldn't start drooling.

With every fleeting glance, another feature came into focus: a ski-ramp nose. A pock-mark on his left cheek. A hint of razor stubble. To say nothing of those devilish, playful, sky-colored eyes with inky pupils darting about, prolonged angled lashes, and eyebrows symmetrically arched. He was becoming more gorgeous by the second. Even his earlobes were perfect.

I had barely finished his face when the bell rang. *Ten minutes already?* Felt like ten seconds.

"Well, so much for that," I said.

Clark leaned over. "Let's see what you've got." I wanted to cover up the page—the sketch looked scribbled, the line wobbly. Amateur. And the face bore no resemblance to him.

"Sorry," I said.

"For what?" he asked. "It's good."

"It looks nothing like you."

"I think it looks a lot like me."

Was he being polite, or honest? I assumed Choice A.

"Plus my dull pencil," I said. *Have I always said such idiotic things throughout my entire life?*

"Better than anything I can do in under ten minutes," he said. I smiled.

We stood up to file out of the room. "Shall I walk with you to class again, Wylie Baker?"

Yes, yes, dear God, YES!

"If you want," I said.

The two of us walked down the hallway and stopped at the corner, near my Science classroom.

"Don't forget, you owe me a letter. And I want it before detention today."

"How am I going to get it to you?" I asked. "I don't even know your class schedule."

"I'll text you where my locker is and the combination and you can drop it off there."

"I'll try," I said.

His blue eyes twinkled as he grinned. "See you, Wylie."

I grinned back, leaning back against the wall to steady myself—every part of me was trembling with giddy glee. "See you, Clark."

I spent the next thirty minutes furtively writing back to Clark and praying I wouldn't get caught. It took every ounce of willpower not to check my silenced phone for his text message.

> *Dear Clark,*
>
> *I'm in Science class right now praying Webber doesn't catch me and make me read this to the class as humiliating punishment. Therefore, it'll probably be a short letter with messy handwriting because I'm writing it so fast. Plus I've never written a letter before, so this one will probably suck. Sorry.*
>
> *I guess I'll just answer your points in order. Sorry if that's boring. I am totally terrified of getting caught right now.*
>
> *Sometimes I think it would have been cool to grow up in the 80s. (People still wrote letters then.) Everyone thinks the clothes were ridiculous, but I love them, especially the men's clothes. I also love the hair, which probably makes me even more crazy. Even some mullets looked cool. And isn't "mullet" like an awful-sounding word? It's one of those words that makes you hate the thing as much as you hate the word, like "vomit." Sorry, that was probably a gross example.*

I considered crossing that last part out, but he'd see it anyway.

I don't know if I want to be a graphic designer. If I did I'd want to design lipstick tubes or something cool like that. Lately I've gotten so into doing hair and makeup.

Where I was last September was meeting my you-know-who for the first time. I tracked him down with the help of my sister and had the crazy idea to go to Massachusetts by myself and show up at his doorstep without my parents knowing. He had no clue who I was. When I look back now, I can't believe I did it, considering he could've been a serial killer or something.

I've never had a boyfriend. I guess that makes me some sort of loser.

Not that I care about sports, but my parents are originally from Long Island (so is you-know-who and his wife) and my parents root for the Mets and the Giants. I think "YKW" is a Mets fan and his wife is a Yankees fan (don't hold it against her, she's cool). I don't even know the basketball teams. I guess that makes me dead to you. (So then why am I even bothering with this letter?) My dad plays golf occasionally. He taught me how to play, and I even caddied for him a few times but I was bored beyond belief. Besides, caddying is way more work than it seems. So is walking an entire golf course.

You're the first Clark I know. I don't think it's a nerdy name, especially when you compare it to the name Wylie. I was named after my great-grandfather. Seems weird to name a girl after a dead guy, but obviously I come from a messed up family.

I'd better go now, WEBBER IS LOOKING RIGHT AT ME!

Wylie

P.S. I keep forgetting to ask, but do you know my sister, Patricia Baker? She's a senior too, and goes by Trish. I haven't asked her if she knows you.

After class I checked my phone, and sure enough, Clark sent a text, which sent my heart beating double-time: *McNally is staring me down. Gotta go before she takes phone. Can you leave letter in art room?*

On the way to my last class, I detoured to the art room, took out the tri-folded notebook paper, and hid it behind my canvas board on the easel. Then I texted Clark: *Look behind the easel. I don't have to tell you which one.*

Around eight p.m. that night, I got yet another text from Clark: *Let's pretend we live in the 80s where there was no texting. We'll only write letters.*

I texted back: *Pretty sure they had telephones in the 80s.*

Seconds later, my phone rang. *Clark!*

"Hello?" I said, my voice going up in pitch like, three times.

"They didn't have cellphones," said Clark without even saying hi back. "Let's be true to the times. Grody to the max and all that shit."

I laughed. "Not even Skype or FaceTime or SnapChat?"

"Nope. Letters all the way. Oh, and even though it's so wrong that you don't like sports, I've decided not to make you dead to me."

"Totally tubular," I played along. *Ohmigod, would this goofy grin ever go away?*

"So then, tomorrow?" he asked.

"Same Bat-time, same Bat-channel." I could've sworn he smiled. As if I could see it right through the phone. I was bummed he wasn't even up for SnapChat.

I put my phone away and wrote Clark another letter so he'd have one to read for tomorrow's detention. And somehow I knew he was writing me another one at the very same time.

I completely forgot to text Roxanne and Bottsy.

Right before I went to bed, my phone pinged. I held it up and read: *Breaking no-texting rule just to tell you this: YOU ARE NOT A LOSER. Good night, Wylie Baker.*

Pretty sure I fell asleep with that goofy grin.

Chapter Nine

Dear Wylie,

First of all, you are totally funny. Second of all, your handwriting isn't any messier than mine, which probably came out as an insult rather than a compliment. (Do you find that your hand cramps up quickly when you hand-write as opposed to type? Mine does. Our generation is so pathetic.) Third of all, since you like your biological dad's wife so much, I'll excuse the fact that she's a Yankee fan and not make her dead to me. You're a good character reference.

You're not a loser because you've never had a boyfriend. It's not like you're, say, fifty, and never had a boyfriend. You're sixteen. Sixteen is the perfect time to start dating someone, I think. Don't sweat it. There's plenty of time. Go out and have fun with your friends and just be your cool self.

Your friend,

Clark

P.S. I do know your sister in that I know her name and her face. We've been in some classes together over the years. She usually sits behind me, you know, alphabetical order.

Funny that I didn't put the two of you together as related. Is she your half-sister?

P.P.S. Have we talked TV shows yet?

Dear Clark,

My sister is actually my stepsister, so that's probably why you didn't put us together. We don't look anything alike (why should we if we're not related?). I call my stepdad "dad" and Trish "my sister," because that's who've they've been for almost my entire life. I get along with both of them great, like normal family members get along, and of course I love them. But I've grown to love David and Andi as well. The more I get to know David, the more he feels like a father to me, almost as much as my regular dad. Like, it feels right on the inside, if that makes any sense. Do you have any brothers or sisters?

I'm glad you don't think I'm a loser. A lot of my friends have already dated or are dating someone. I've hung out with guys, mostly in group situations and a couple of times one-on-one, but I wouldn't call any of them dates. And one of my best friends is a guy, but that's it. I don't want to date just anyone. I want to be with someone special. That probably sounds like stupid fairytale stuff.

I'm hopefully getting my driver's permit when school ends. Totally nervous! I suck at taking tests. Once I get it, look out, world (ha ha ha). I'm taking Driver's Ed over the summer. I doubt I'll be getting a car anytime soon, though. And even when I do, it'll probably be a used one, like yours was. My dream car is a Fiat. Either that or a Mini Cooper. Aren't they the most adorable things?

I feel like I'm rambling. Like I have nothing intelligent

or thoughtful to say. I wish I could be philosophical too. I don't care about politics or religion, I don't like sports (again, sorry), and I don't read as much as I should (hey, weren't you supposed to make up a reading list for me)? So what do I like? The usual girl stuff, I guess. Hair. Makeup. Clothes. Shoes. And drawing and painting. All the stuff I've already told you about. I love going to museums. They're such peaceful places, except when there's a big exhibit and everyone is there. You want to know something cool? David loves museums too. One of our first outings together was at the Boston Museum of Fine Arts. Isn't that totally cool?

Can I just tell you that I love that I can talk to you about David? I can talk to my besties too, but it's not the same as when I talk to you. I'm not sure why.

No, we haven't talked TV shows yet. What are your favorites? Most of them seem pretty stupid to me.

Wylie

Dear Wylie
I have to keep this one short, but here's the reading list:
Hitchhiker's Guide to the Galaxy
2001: A Space Odyssey
Wool
The Martian
A Wrinkle in Time
The entire Harry Potter series
Everything Stephen King has ever written, but start with Carrie

That should keep you busy for now. If you like anything by James Patterson, Nicholas Sparks, or werewolves with buffed pectorals and abs then...well, you can finish the sentence by now.

And by the way, if you think most TV shows are stupid, then you're totally watching the wrong shows. Homeland, The Wire, House of Cards, Game of Thrones, Leverage, Suits, Dexter, Walking Dead, True Detective, Breaking Bad, Mad Men (oh my God, Wylie, MAKE IT STOP!), there's just too many to choose from. I swear, if I could I'd drop out of school and spend my days watching these shows, I'd get a perfectly decent, if not better, education. If I got paid for it, well, then, I'd win at life.

Your friend,
Clark
P.S. I have a little brother who's graduating middle school this year.
P.P.S. What has your family life been like since meeting David?

Dear Clark,
Both David and Andi say I was brave to find him. My mother still hasn't forgiven me for turning everyone's life upside down. My dad sometimes looks like he's about to cry. One minute Trish seems like she doesn't care, the next minute she seems weirded out by it all. And I guess that's the way it's been for me too. There are days when I feel way closer to David and Andi than I do my parents. And then I feel horribly guilty for feeling that way, because they've been good parents and I know it hurts them.
Wylie

Dear Wylie,
Add me to the list of those who think you were brave to

go meet your dad in person. Although you probably were also stupid in a crazy way. Like you said, you didn't know anything about him, and he could've been some psychopath. But given how cool you are, the odds of that had to be close to nil, so you made the right call. Did he totally freak out when he first met you? I can't fathom a kid showing up on my doorstep and telling me I fathered her. (Sorry to call you a "kid" – I'm just doing the hypothetical here.)

Anyway, I have to cut this short because I have to go to work. Your uncle's mantra is: "Early is on time, and on time is late."

Your friend,
Clark

I quickly re-folded Clark's latest letter as Roxanne set her lunch tray at the table and took a seat across from me and Bottsy, next to Caitlyn.

"Annette told me she saw you walking to Science with Clark Anderson for the last four days," said Roxanne.

I nearly choked on my Nutella and banana sandwich. "You know Clark Anderson?"

"He's a senior. Was practically engaged to Lulu Lawrence until they broke up last year. The question, however, is how do *you* know him, and what are you doing hanging out with a senior? Or, more to the point, what is a senior doing hanging out with you? And why did I have to hear about it from Annette?"

How did she know these things? I'd never heard of him prior to detention—and all this time he's been in my Study Hall class! And Lulu Lawrence was the mystery girlfriend? The one in the YouTube video doing the piano recital?

"What, there's some law that says seniors can't hang out with sophs? And how does Annette know him—come to think of it, how do *you* know him?"

"I don't know, I just do. I mean, I don't know him personally or anything like that, and he probably has no clue I exist. And you haven't answered any of my questions."

There was no way out of this conversation but through it. "He was in detention with me on Monday."

"And you didn't tell me?" said Roxanne.

"What's to tell?" I said, trying to avoid Roxanne's skeptical glare. I was a decent liar when I had to be (or so I thought), but I couldn't get anything past her.

"Um, hel-lo?" said Roxanne. "A senior starts palling around with you and you don't tell your best friend? I'm hurt." Bottsy honed in on his sandwich as if eating it were the most important thing in the room.

"It's really no big deal," I said. "He's like one of those guys you talk to in class because you have no one else to talk to. We're not texting or anything." *At least that much was true, right?* "And like you said, he's a senior. He'll be out of here and forget my name in a month."

She wasn't buying it.

"Clark Anderson is cute in that dorky sort of way," Caitlyn offered. "Like, if he got rid of those glasses and upgraded his wardrobe he'd be kind of a hottie."

Kind of? KIND OF??? Please. What was the expression Andi used? *Total fox.* Clark Anderson was a total fox, glasses or no glasses. Leather biker jacket or no leather biker jacket.

"I guess so," I said.

Roxanne pointed at me accusingly. "You *like* him, don't you."

"I do not," I said, knowing the emphatic denial was only further exposing me.

"Why would you keep that from us?" asked Bottsy. He sounded even more hurt than Roxanne, who just sounded annoyed.

"Maybe because I didn't want to get the third degree, like I'm getting right now. Look, what's the big deal? So I like a senior. So we're hanging out. That's all it is. There was nothing to tell."

I was lying through my teeth. They had a right to be hurt. I didn't know why I'd been keeping it from them. There'd been plenty to tell. Plenty to show too. Had this been a year ago I probably would've showed Roxanne every single letter Clark had given me and we would've scrutinized each one, analyzing them for hidden messages. So what changed? Why didn't I trust the support of the two people I'd known and been friends with since elementary school?

"You want to hang out with Clark Anderson and get your heart stomped on, then be my guest," said Roxanne. "But don't come running to me when it happens. And it *will* happen."

I looked at her, completely baffled. "What is your *problem*, Rox? First you bite my head off and call me dense, now you're acting like you're all jealous of something."

"That's because you *are* dense. You're too dense to see that a perfectly nice guy right in front of you already likes you and you treat him like dirt."

"Who?" I said.

"Who do you think?"

Her eyes went immediately to Bottsy, followed by the rest of ours. Bottsy? *Bottsy likes me as more than a friend? Since when?*

Every molecule in my body froze in disbelief, until one by one the scenes came into focus: all the times he playfully put his arm around me; his asking me to dance with him at my party; the charm bracelet…

Ohmigod, oh, my God!

Bottsy, his mouth clamped shut and his face the shade of a tomato, gave Roxanne the angriest stare I've ever seen from him. I'd never known Bottsy to be truly mad at anyone.

He stood up. "I told you not to say anything," he said to Roxanne so low we barely heard it, grabbed his backpack, and abandoned his lunch and us.

While he was still within earshot, Roxanne, on the verge of tears, jumped up and followed him. "John, wait!"

John? I couldn't remember the last time I'd heard anyone other than a teacher or his parents call him John.

Caitlyn and I stared at each other, shell-shocked.

"You know she's liked him, like, forever," said Caitlyn. "That's why she's been so hostile toward you lately."

WHAT?

"Define 'forever'," I said, my mind utterly blown.

"OK, maybe not 'forever,' but definitely, like, at least the last year. Ever since Annette's party where everyone hooked up with everyone else."

That was the night Bottsy and I had kissed. I'd told Roxanne about it after the fact. She'd seemed fine. Had she kissed him too at some point? Had our kiss actually meant something to Bottsy? If so, then why didn't he tell me sooner? Why didn't Roxanne? Why didn't someone, anyone, tell me *something*?

"I never knew," I said quietly, more to myself than to Caitlyn.

"I think she was too afraid you would tell him, although I guess that's been taken care of now."

How had I not even noticed all this time? Roxanne was right: I must be dense. Worse than that. I am a horrible, horrible friend. But that still didn't justify Roxanne being so mad at me for not telling her about Clark when she kept a whopper of a secret from me. I couldn't help it that Bottsy liked me. I didn't even know. How could she be mad at me for something I had no control over?

"So what are you doing this weekend?" Caitlyn asked, as if the whole drama didn't just happen.

"I'm going up to Massachusetts this weekend," I replied, dazed. I barely even heard myself say it.

"You go up there a lot now," said Caitlyn.

Great. Yet another hole to dig out of because I didn't think before I spoke. "Not *a lot*," I said. "Once every other month, maybe?"

"What's up there, anyway?"

"What are *you* doing, Caitlyn?"

"Saturday I'm going job hunting. Hopefully stores are looking for part-time summer help. Sunday I have to go to my baby cousin's baptism."

Lunch couldn't end soon enough. Nor could the rest of the day, for that matter, with the exception of Study Hall. The idea of just showing up to detention for no reason and hanging out with Clark suddenly tempted me. He was the only person who could take my mind off what had happened with Roxanne and Bottsy.

I could barely sit still when Clark entered Study Hall, his biker jacket replaced with a stylish blazer over yet another graphic T-shirt, distressed black jeans, and motorcycle boots. He had the thick studded leather band around his wrist, below his watch, the one that had caught my eye at my Sweet Sixteen party.

"I have to know where you got that bracelet," I said as I ogled it yet again.

He extended his wrist. "Wanna wear it?"

Only every day for the rest of my life...

"Oh, thanks. Um, no, you wear it. It looks good on you."

He took it off and fastened it on my left wrist. Just the feel of his fingers brushing up against the back of my hand made me break out in a sweat. "Looks good on you too," he said.

I was dying to ask him, *What does this mean? You sign every letter "Your friend," but you don't seem to be acting like a friend. YOU*

JUST PUT YOUR BRACELET ON ME. All because it reminded you of something I liked. Doesn't that mean something? I don't know what felt worse—not knowing when I so clearly should, or perhaps already knowing and not trusting it.

"Oh, I have a new letter for you," I said, and dug into the secret compartment of my purse.

"Good, because I have one for you too."

We exchanged the folded notebook paper, and it occurred to me that we should have nicer stationery. He took mine, put it to his nose, and took a whiff. Then he grinned. "Smells like you."

I didn't know whether I was going to spontaneously combust or dissolve into a sloshy pool of mush. And what did I smell like?

I put his letter to my nose in imitation, and inhaled. Smelled like pen ink, much to my disappointment.

"I'm kind of sorry your detention is almost over," I said. "I like these letters."

"Me too," he replied. "We should definitely keep writing them. I've never gotten to know someone this way."

"Me neither," I said.

The magnitude hit me instantly: *We were getting to know each other.* It wasn't just about favorite colors and movies. It was about finding out who we really were, what made us tick. To say nothing of the fact that he *wanted* to get to know me. But was that all it was ever going to be? Were we ever going to *go* anywhere or *do* anything? Were we ever going to grab a coffee after school or see a movie on the weekend? Was he ever going to hug me or kiss me or put his arm around me? Were we ever going to text or SnapChat until all hours of the night? Was writing letters enough? Did it meet the standard requirement for being friends? Did it count as being in a relationship with someone if you didn't actually *see* or *talk* to them?

However, writing letters to Clark required more care and effort than texting. I took time to think about how to express myself, to choose what I wanted to share, and not just those typical getting-to-know-you questions. I wanted to think about the *words*. All those things Andi taught me were starting to make sense: a purpose, an audience, a medium. What did she call it? *A rhetorical situation.* That had to be a good thing, right?

Study Hall passed in fast motion yet again—figured, the one class I *didn't* want to end so quickly. Clark and I spent it making lists of our favorite and hated words (an idea I'd gotten from Andi; he loved it) and exchanging them, trying not to laugh too loud. After the bell rang and as we filed out, Clark said, "So what are you doing this weekend, Wylie Baker?"

My heartbeat sped up—*ohmigod, was he about to ask me on a date?* "Oh, I'm actually going up to see David and Andi. I haven't visited them in a long time. I mean, they came to my Sweet Sixteen party a couple of weeks ago—"

Clark interrupted me: "Consider the bracelet your birthday present."

That did it. I was *never* going to remove that bracelet, except for when I showered.

"Thanks," I said, twisting and turning my wrist to admire it. *Play it cool, Wylie Jean. Don't let him know you're about to jump out of your socks with glee.* "Anyway, they've got a new house and I'm looking forward to seeing it and hanging out with them."

"That's great," said Clark. Was it just wishful thinking, or did he sound disappointed?

"You doing anything fun?" I asked.

"Nah. Hey, I gotta run; otherwise I'll get in trouble. I've been getting to class after the bell every day this week."

So, he wasn't going to ask me out. The disappointment practically choked me.

"Had I known I wouldn't have let you walk with me to class."

"No worries," he said. "Have a good weekend."

"You too," I said.

Two whole days without seeing Clark Anderson? How was I ever going to get through it? Although really, what difference did it make if he had no interest in seeing me?

Chapter Ten

After school I entered my house, bounded up the stairs, dumped my purse and backpack on my bed, and sat at my laptop, where I Googled *Lulu Lawrence*. The search produced a page of hits, including photos. She had Asian features with luscious jet-black hair that you see on shampoo commercials, a body and outfits straight off a runway (I'll bet she wore matching lace underwear *every day*), and the whitest, straightest teeth I'd ever seen. Aside from her Facebook page, a ton of links boasting her accolades appeared—valedictorian of Gerald Ford High School, National Merit Scholar, Regional Scholar, an award from some entrepreneurial society, President of Key Club, youngest member inducted into the local Rotary Club, Harvard freshman, and more. In addition to the duet with Clark, there was a YouTube video of her playing some classical piece during a piano recital from a couple of years ago, which would have made her at least sixteen. She looked way older at sixteen than I do. She *acted* older. Of course, she was perfect, not a note out of place. Even her posture sitting at the piano was straight and proper and commanding.

No wonder Clark went bonkers for her. What on earth was he doing even being friends with me? There was *no way* I could measure up. Like, not even close. I'll bet she could even draw and paint. She was probably perfect when it came to sex too. Like, they probably did it all the time, and she probably taught him everything he knows.

I Googled both Clark and Lulu's names together and found a bunch of photos of the two of them together looking very much like David and Andi—hands all over each other, goo-goo eyes, and totally in love. My guess was that there were tons more but they probably all got deleted post-breakup.

Meanwhile, my phone was tortuously silent. Still no text messages from Roxanne or Bottsy. We'd had our spats before. They usually blew over an hour or two later, a day at most. But this was more than a spat, and I had no idea what to do about it. Every time I thought about sending one to either one of them, I couldn't think of what to say. Maybe I should write Roxanne a letter? Or maybe I could talk to my mom. But I don't know, something about it seemed too embarrassing.

That night at dinner, Trish piped up. "So what's this I hear about you being practically joined at the hip with Clark Anderson?"

I nearly spit out my peas. Why did these things always happen when I was eating?

"Oh please, you too? Rox grilled me earlier as well. What is the big deal with my talking to a senior?"

"You're dating a senior?" said Mom. "Since when?"

"I am not 'dating' anyone!" I said. "I said 'talking' to one. We're in Study Hall together."

"Well, we've been in a bunch of classes together and barely said more than two words to each other, although he did let me cheat off him on a test once."

"I'll pretend I didn't hear that," said Dad.

"Well, I'm not dating him," I reiterated.

"Then where'd you get *that*?" accused Trish, eyeing the studded leather band Clark had put on my wrist during Study Hall. Now I was completely mortified, my face burning and my palms sweating as I yanked my wrist out of view and hid it under the table. Trish laughed and pointed at me in a teasing way. "Not dating, my ass!"

"I swear to God, I'm not!"

"OK," said Mom to Trish, "Enough."

"Hey, you've got my blessing. He's a got that mix of cute plus geek working for him. Plus the cool biker jacket. Although you know me, I prefer the more hunky type. He was really serious with Lulu Lawrence, though. Like, wanted to marry her. And she crushed him. You should know that."

Again with Lulu Lawrence? I instantly lost my appetite.

"May I be excused?" I asked.

My parents granted permission. As I stood up, my mother said, "Oh, Wylie, before you go, there's been a change of plans. David and Andi are coming here tomorrow."

Geez, kick me while I'm down, why don't you!

"Why?"

"Because I have to work and Dad has to take his car to the shop."

"I'm sure one of them offered to pick me up and take me back themselves," I said.

"Well, they already agreed to come here, so it's settled," said Mom.

"And you didn't think to ask what *I* wanted before you 'settled' it? Or did you just not care?"

"Wylie, you can do what you want when you're eighteen, but for now we still make decisions for you, and David and Andi defer to *us*, understand?" said Dad.

Dad's words rang between my ears: *I'm sorry this isn't enough for you.* What, was he trying to prove that it was? That it could be?

"No, I *don't* understand. I may not be eighteen yet, but I'm not twelve either."

"Go to your room," said Mom.

"With pleasure," I said, and skulked out of the kitchen to my room.

> *Dear Clark,*
> *I hate being the youngest. I hate not being eighteen. I hate that my parents still get to make decisions on my behalf without consulting me first and expect me to just obediently go along with it. I hate that both of my best friends aren't speaking to me right now. I hate that you're not here right now for me to vent to personally. I hate that you're two years older than me and everyone acts like you're twenty years older. I hate that you're graduating this year and I'm not. I hate Lulu Lawrence for getting there first. I hate that I'm writing you a letter I can't give you. I hate how much I miss you right now, how I'm dying to put my arms around you and feel you hugging me, how I'm dying to know what it's like to kiss you right this very second, how I can still feel the warmth of your skin as it brushed against mine when you put that leather bracelet on me. I'm in love with you, Clark. God, I've only known you for a few days and I'm so in love with you and it hurts so much because I don't think you love me back in that way. Please tell me that you do.*
> *Love, Wylie*

I folded the paper in threes, shoved it under my pillow, dropped my head on it, and cried.

I didn't realize I'd fallen asleep until the pounding on my door jolted me awake. Trish poked her head in and held up a package of Twizzlers. "Truce?" she said.

I motioned her in and held out my hand. She tossed the Twizzlers to me and I caught it, ripping the package open and pulling one out with my teeth.

"Sorry I teased you about Clark," she said.

I shrugged and chewed. "S'ok."

"Based on what little interaction I've had, he seems really nice." She sat on my bed, and the two of us faced each other, cross-legged.

I decided to confide in Trish. She was my sister, after all. "I do really like him," I said.

"Yeah, it's written all over your face."

"Wonderful," I said. "It's worse than that. I'm always a total nervous wreck when I'm around him. And when I'm not around him I can't stop thinking about him. Can't concentrate on anything else for more than two seconds. I'm like, Clark-obsessed. I hate that. I never wanted to be one of those girls who can't breathe without mentioning his name."

"It does seem unlike you. Then again, I don't think I was any different with my first crush."

Was that all this was? A crush? It felt like more. I certainly wanted it to be more.

"Does he like you back?" she asked.

"I honestly don't know. Sometimes I think he does and sometimes I think he's just being friendly."

"Don't get your hopes up," she said. "I mean, he may really like you—what's not to like?" She smiled and gave me a playful punch. "But if he's going away to college next year and you're staying behind, it's really hard to sustain any kind of relationship no matter how much he likes you. Besides, the age gap between sixteen and eighteen is way larger than, say, twenty and twenty-two. Don't ask me why, but it is. Maybe you should just forget about him."

"Wow. Good pep talk, Trish."

"Honestly, Wylie, I don't want you to get hurt. I'm sorry it sounds like I'm not being supportive, but I really am. And I meant what I said about him and Lulu. I wouldn't want you to be nothing more than a rebound for him. Whatever you do, don't sleep with him. You'll get even more attached, and he'll go off and dump you for someone in college."

Whoa—sleep with him? I decided to ignore that and asked my next question.

"Did you know Lulu?" I asked.

"A little bit. She was in all honors, so the only time we were in class together was Phys Ed one quarter last year. Other than that she was way out of my league. She graduated a year early last year."

"What was she like?"

"A genius, for one thing," said Trish. "They disqualified her from entering the last science fair because she'd won every year for the last five years or something crazy like that. Her parents are rich, so she wore all designer clothes. Depending on whom you talk to, some called her stuck up while others said she was really down-to-earth. She is definitely a know-it-all—like, literally, she knows everything. And she's beautiful."

"Thanks, I feel so much better now."

Trish ignored my sarcasm. "Now what's got you so upset about David and Andi coming here rather than you going there?"

"I just wanted to get out of here for a change, and I hate that they all make decisions about me without my having any say in it."

"Well, I think this is Janine and Dad's way of keeping their eye on David and Andi. They're still afraid of them, you know. There's some big secret that they're trying to keep."

Trish used to call my mother "Mom," but when she was about fifteen she reverted to "Janine," after reconnecting with her biological mother, whom I've never met. I remembered how awkward it was to hear it. Mom had freaked the first time she did so, as did Dad.

Apparently he and Trish's mom had an ugly divorce. I've never called my dad anything other than Dad, and yet I haven't been able to call my biological father anything other than his first name.

"Tell me about it," I said. "I wish they'd see that keeping it from me is way worse than what the actual secret is." I leaned in and asked in a hushed voice, "You don't know what it is, do you?"

She shook her head. At that moment I considered asking Trish to put her sleuthing skills to work again and help me find out. Come to think of it, why had I never asked her before? Was it possible I was more afraid of what I would find?

Trish stood up, closed and locked my bedroom door, and returned to the bed. "Do you think maybe David got your mom pregnant against her will?"

"Wait—you mean, like, he date-raped her?" I said the words in a whisper, they were so repugnant to me.

Trish nodded.

I put a hand to my mouth as a wave of nausea ran through me. Could feel the blood drain from my face.

Oh God. Oh please, no.

I couldn't bear to think he could be such a monster. But it would explain why Mom had such a chilly demeanor toward him, and never wanted him to know about me, or tell me about him.

But if it was true, then how could my mom get involved with someone like that? How could Andi *marry* someone like that? Both were way too smart to be with someone who would do something so despicable. Although I remembered Andi telling me when she and I first met about how he was a different person back when she first knew him. Still, how do you let something like that slip by and act like it was no big deal, all in the past? Or maybe *she* didn't know?

All this time, I've liked David. More than that. How could

someone as nice as that, someone I really did love, do something so awful to my mother? *It just couldn't be.*

I shuddered. "I suddenly feel like I need a shower," I said to Trish.

Mom came to my room close to ten thirty to say goodnight.

"Wylie, honey, I know you're getting older, but you have to trust that when Dad and I make decisions for you, we make them with your best interest at heart. We may make mistakes sometimes, but never with the intention to hurt you."

"Mom, were you date-raped?"

My mother gasped in horror. "What?"

"Is that how you got pregnant with me? Did David force you to have sex against your will?"

"*Absolutely not.* Where on earth did you get that idea?"

I didn't want to rat out Trish and get her in trouble, so I said, "I don't know, I just thought maybe that's why you're all secretive about David's past."

"Wylie, what David and I did was one hundred percent consensual. He would never do anything like that to a woman. *Ever.*"

I was more than relieved to hear this, although it still didn't appease my frustration. "Then why do you still have such a problem with him? Why can't I go stay with them for the weekend?"

Mom sighed. "He's just…He wasn't the man I wanted to conceive a child with, OK? It doesn't mean I didn't want you, and that I wouldn't do it all over again just to have you, but…I just wish it wasn't such a complicated situation."

She didn't answer my question.

"And as for this weekend," she continued, "I'm concerned about your focus lately, what with detention and your suddenly wanting to switch schools."

Now it made sense. She probably thought I was going to secretly enroll myself in the Massachusetts school while I was there. "Dad told you?"

"Of course he told me," she said before adding, "And now there's this boy…"

"I told you, it's nothing!" I wasn't fooling her any more than I'd fooled Roxanne. Seemed strange to refer to Clark as a "boy" when he seemed so much older.

"I don't have a problem with you dating as long as you tell Dad and me who he is and we get to meet him and he's not too old or into anything unacceptable. But you can't let your whole life revolve around a boy. You've got to start thinking about colleges now, and I want you to keep your head in the game."

"For the last time, I am *not* dating him! And how does going to Northampton this weekend as opposed to being stuck in stupid West Hartford keep my head *out* of the game?"

Mom shook her head. "Wylie…" she started, but found no other words. She hugged me goodnight, and turned off the light on her way out of my room. I didn't even get to tell her or Trish about what happened with Roxanne and Bottsy. There was no room to jump in.

As I stared at the ceiling, waiting to fall asleep, I thought of a possible silver lining to my being stuck in Hartford for the weekend with no friends. *Maybe there was a way I could see Clark.*

Chapter Eleven

David and Andi arrived around eleven o'clock the next morning. Andi's dark hair color from the party was already faded, and I even detected a bit of gray at the roots. She wore a vertically striped poplin shirt with three-quarter sleeves, dark blue boot-cut jeans, and clogs. David was dressed in what looked to be a finely knit button-down shirt paired with classic Levi's jeans and Steve Madden shoes. He looked ready for a photo shoot for a Macy's ad. Although I was glad to see them, I still couldn't hide my disappointment about not getting away for the weekend. Besides, there was never anything to do around here. The three of us wound up seeing a movie and going to IHOP afterward. We made small talk about the movie all the way to IHOP and until the server took our orders. (Maybe I could tell *them* about Roxanne and Bottsy?)

"Everything OK at school?" asked Andi after we ordered.

I shrugged. "I guess. My English teacher wants me to do an essay about that reading you sent me. Said he'd give me extra credit."

"That's great, Wylie." Andi smiled. "You should do it."

Before I could ask her why she'd sent it, David asked, "Which reading is that?"

" 'Letter from Birmingham Jail'," said Andi.

David raised his eyebrows. "That's rather impressive." He added,

"If I recall, that was one of the readings you gave me back in another lifetime." Then he winked at her. I couldn't help but notice the lines protruding from the corners of his eyes—"crow's feet" they're called, I think. Adults seemed to complain about them, but to me they enhanced a smile or a wink. Especially with David. I wondered if those would be my eyes when I reached his age.

"You tutored David?" I said.

"Something like that," said Andi. "It was a long, long time ago." She gave him a look I couldn't quite read, and returned her attention to me. "How are you doing with the reading?"

"It's really hard. Plus, I don't see the relevance to—" I cut myself off and settled instead on "...anything."

I'm pretty sure Andi read my mind. "We can talk about it during our next Skype session," she said.

David pointed to my wrist. "Where'd you get that?" he said of Clark's studded leather bracelet. My pulse quickened as I twirled my wrist to admire it once again. Before I could answer, he said, "Very retro. I guess your eighties party made quite an impression on you."

"Oh, Andi, I forgot to tell you—I know someone who's starting Edmund College in the fall," I said.

Her eyes flickered and faded all in the span of a split second. "That's great. Edmund is a really good liberal-arts school. Excellent faculty and efficient administrators. Rivals NU."

David put his arm around her and pulled her to him, then kissed her near the temple of her forehead.

"Do you know anybody there?" I asked, and then realized how stupid the question was. "I mean, do you still—" I started.

Andi finished for me as forgiveness of my stupidity. "I do. Sam's colleagues. If your friend wants the lowdown on anything, let me know and I'll put her in touch with them."

"Oh, it's a *he*, actually," I said, and blushed as the corners of my mouth twitched. If only there was a way to control that.

David raised his eyebrows again and seemed about to say something, when Andi quickly chimed in, "Well, tell him I'll connect him to the right people if he's interested."

I hoped she was getting the thank-you-for-not-asking-me-about-the-*he* message I was telepathically sending her. Judging by the way her eyes seemed to be saying *you're welcome, I've been there*, I'd say she did.

The server brought our orders about five minutes later. We were in the middle of eating when I heard, "Wylie?" I looked up, my mouth stuffed with pancakes.

Christina.

She was standing in front of our booth with Hillary and two other girls I knew, Erica and Ashley, smiling the fakest, meanest, out-to-get-me-est smile you could smile. "What a surprise," she said. Then she turned to David and Andi. "Hello, do you remember me? From the party? I'm Christina."

David and Andi nodded and acknowledged her politely.

I forced a swallow. "What are you doing here, Dickerson?" I said, not even bothering to fake cordiality.

"Same as you, getting a bite to eat." She re-introduced Hillary, followed by Ashley and Erica, to David and Andi, and then turned her attention yet again to David. "I almost didn't recognize you out of costume."

I tried to give Andi a light kick under the table to let her know that this was the ex-friend bothering me. She seemed to know despite my kicking.

"Well, we don't want to keep you from your table. And we're on a bit of a tight schedule," said Andi, who fixed her eyes on Christina long enough to make Christina uncomfortable. For someone who's never had kids, Andi sometimes acts like a lion protecting her cubs. No wonder her students love her. I'll bet she sticks up for them all the time. Christina and company said their goodbyes, a scowl behind their smiles, as Erica muttered, "Well, she's rude," in reference to Andi, loud enough for us to hear as they walked away. From my peripheral vision I watched them slide into their seats three booths back on the other side of restaurant, within perfect eyeshot of David. We all pretended not to hear Erica's comment, but *Ugh.*

David turned to Andi. "We're on a tight schedule?" he asked.

"How on earth did they know I was here?" I asked. "It's just too convenient to be a coincidence."

"What's going on?" said David. "They're your friends, aren't they?"

"Not anymore," I said.

"How come?"

I looked at Andi and once again tried to communicate with her non-verbally: *Please don't tell him.* She didn't quite get the message this time. "Let's talk about this later, when we get in the car. In fact, I'm full. How about you, Wylie?"

I nodded, even though I hadn't even eaten half of my pancakes. Didn't matter. I was sick to my stomach now.

"Dev, would you mind getting the check?" asked Andi. It still threw me sometimes when Andi called him that. They're so used to it that I guess they don't even notice it.

David and Andi were having their own mental conversation, I could tell. He got our server's attention and asked for the check. As the three of us stood up to leave, I looked back at Hillary and Christina, looking at me triumphantly. Christina waved her phone at me, and then I knew: *Shit—she'd gotten another picture of him! How had she done it with none of us noticing? How did I not even anticipate that she would?*

And then it hit me: this wasn't about Christina being David-obsessed. She was over that. No, this was about her knowing that she had something on me, something that made me uncomfortable.

That she could match my secret with one of her own. What if she'd actually found out he was my biological father and was waiting for the perfect moment to out me?

This time I imagined myself dumping the carafe of boysenberry syrup on her head. I even considered paying the server to do it.

While David was paying for the meal, Andi whispered to me, "You've got to tell him about the bullying and the things Christina is saying, Wylie. He doesn't like when secrets are kept from him. Especially concerning you."

Seriously? Then maybe he shouldn't keep them from me, I wanted to say.

When we got out to the car, David said, "Would you mind telling me what that was all about?" He sounded just like a father would.

"It's nothing," I said. "Christina is poking her nose into my business, that's all."

"You mean *our* business," said David. Nice to know that we understood each other.

"Something like that," I said. "Don't worry, I haven't told her anything. Roxanne and Bottsy are still the only friends who know." *And Clark.* Although now that Roxanne was all mad at me and I knew the truth about Bottsy liking me, who knew whether they'd keep my secret too? Were they even still my friends?

No. They would never tell. Not in a million years. Even if they hated my guts.

"You OK?" said Andi. "You just went pale."

"I want to go home," I said, tears stinging my eyes. "I'm sorry."

"You have nothing to apologize for, Wylie," said David. He put his arm around me and pulled me into a hug. "If anyone's sorry, it's me."

"For what?" I asked.

His eyes went dark, and his body looked physically restrained. "I just am."

"You know I wanted to come to you guys for the weekend, right?" I said. "I want to make sure you know that this wasn't my idea. This wouldn't have happened if I'd had a say in my own life."

Andi leaned against the car, looking at the ground, her mouth clamped shut. I really wanted to talk to her one-on-one—about Clark, Roxanne, Bottsy, my whole miserable life—but I knew David would feel left out if I confided in her rather than him.

How was it possible to feel so alone when you're in the presence of people who do everything they can to make you feel special?

When David and Andi dropped me back at my house and pulled away, I went up to my room, ignoring my mother asking how my day was, locked myself in my room, and texted Clark.

You around? I know you prefer letters, but I kind of need to talk to you.

A god-awful long five minutes later, Clark texted me back. *As a matter of fact, I am. I can meet you, if you want. Where are you?*

My heart went into Zumba mode. I texted back: *Home.* And followed with my address in case he forgot.

You're not in Massachusetts?

No. Long story. Will tell you later.

My phone pinged again. *Um, *I'm* in Massachusetts. Thought I'd scout for housing this weekend.*

Holy crap on a cracker!

No way it was a coincidence that he chose this particular weekend to go up to Northampton when he knew I was supposed to be there, was it? Was he hoping to run into me? Was he going to call me and try to get together? God, how I would've preferred to run into *him* today.

What now? Should I ask him to come back to Connecticut? Should I play it cool and not mention anything about it?

I texted back: *When are you coming back?*

Tomorrow night. I've got appointments to see apartments all day tomorrow.

Figures.

Clark followed up with: *We can still talk if you want. You can call me.*

Another wave of loneliness crashed over me, along with a jellyfish sting of disappointment for good measure.

I typed, *It's ok. Just stupid stuff.*

Was I crazy? Why not talk on the phone?

Because I'm an inarticulate, stupid sophomore who can't even play "Chopsticks" on the piano, that's why.

Good luck with your apartment hunting.

He texted back: *You sure you're ok?*

I tapped the letters: *See you Monday with a letter.*

Ok

My phone pinged a second later. *((hugs))*

I burst into tears.

Chapter Twelve

I spent Sunday moping around the house, catching up on my homework, re-reading all of Clark's letters from the past week, deleting all photos of my party with Christina and Hillary in them, and trying to forget the fact that both Roxanne and Bottsy were ignoring my texts. I considered texting Clark to find out how his apartment search went, but I didn't want to be some puppy that followed him around—it was bad enough that I thought about him twenty-four-seven. Seriously, what was wrong with me? I also remembered what Trish said about getting involved with him—what was the point if he wasn't going to be here next year? Every time I tried to write a letter to him revealing how I felt about him, I wound up tearing it to shreds.

Monday brought a new form of hell: photos of me—puffed cheeks full of pancakes from Saturday's IHOP visit, sweating in Phys Ed, exiting the Girls Room, my forehead scrunched up in mid-laugh at lunch (who knows when Christina got that considering she's never there and I haven't been laughing much lately—assuming it was Christina who took the photo) taped to my locker door. Caitlyn told me that Christina put all these photos in an album on Facebook and Instagram and titled it WYLIE UNHINGED along with the caption "Shares encouraged." Caitlyn said it was up to ten shares, last time she checked.

It was becoming increasingly difficult to ignore her childish pranks. Worse still, they were finally getting to me.

Neither Roxanne nor Bottsy showed up to lunch. When I saw either one of them in the hallway, they avoided eye contact. It killed me not to see their smiling faces, to have to be so awkward around them. It killed me not to be the me I was when I was with them. The me I didn't have to think about or apologize for. I wound up going to the art room—it was unoccupied during lunch periods, and Mrs. Howard kept it unlocked. She'd also signed a de facto hall pass for those times I wanted extra time to work on a project—I was one of her "special students" who warranted such privileges because I was trustworthy, she'd said. Plus, I didn't take advantage of this privilege except when I was engrossed in a painting, or when Roxanne or any of my other lunch friends were absent.

I put the finishing touches on the still-life painting I'd started prior to detention, put everything back when I was finished, and closed the door behind me.

All day I drifted in and out of class aimlessly, my lips clamped tightly together in attempt to avoid giving Christina and her lackeys the satisfaction of seeing me upset. When I arrived at Study Hall, Clark was waiting for me next to the doorway. He grabbed me by the hand, and a thousand skyrockets shot off in my body.

"Come on," he said, looking to his left and right.

"Where are we going?" I asked.

He pulled me out a side door into a back lot, where his car was parked. "We're taking the rest of the day off."

"Clark, you just finished two weeks of detention for cutting classes. Now you're going to do it all over again?"

He started the engine and sped out of the parking lot onto a side street. "What can I say? I'm a glutton for punishment."

"Didn't you say you wouldn't graduate if you cut any more classes?"

"Well, technically, if I got *caught* cutting any more classes."

I wasn't comforted by this technicality.

"I'll take my chances," he said. "You're not mad that I've made you a fugitive too, are you?"

Honestly, I was invigorated.

"I'll live," I said. "But why?"

"You sounded like you really needed a friend the other night. I was going to call you, but I had a feeling it wasn't the same as being there in person. So I figured I'd take you someplace where just the two of us could talk."

Ohmigod, oh, my God, YES!

"Why not wait until after school?" I asked.

"Do you really want to wait until after school?"

"Not really."

He turned on his car stereo and blasted Adam Ant just for me.

"So where are we going?" I asked.

"You'll see," he said. His grin was so mischievous, and I had to force myself not to gawk at him with goo-goo eyes.

We arrived at the rose gardens in Elizabeth Park. The day was perfect for it—sunny and mild and practically empty considering it was a Monday, save for a few senior citizens or moms with strollers. I was afraid someone would question why two teenagers were walking the grounds during school hours, but no one seemed to notice us. As we entered the park, Clark said, "So tell me all your troubles, Wylie Baker."

"Why do you always say my first and last name together like that? I'm curious, not complaining."

"Because it's fun. Now, that can't be what's bothering you. Spill it."

And spill it I did. I rambled on about my parents changing plans with David and Andi on me, Roxanne and Bottsy not speaking to me, running into Christina at IHOP and her campaign to destroy me, the secrecy surrounding David's past, and my usual moaning about how much Ford High School sucks. Might as well tell him how much of a loser I really am—he would've found out sooner or later anyway.

"Maybe you can graduate a year early," he suggested.

"My grades aren't good enough for that." *Who does he think I am, Lulu Lawrence?*

"Summer school? I think the community college lets you do all your one-oh-one classes over the summer in lieu of AP courses if your grades are good enough."

"One-oh-one classes?" I asked.

"All the courses you take during your freshman year of college. They're like an overview of the subject—Biology one-oh-one, Psychology one-oh-one, English one-oh-one, and so on."

Duh. How could I not know that? One more reason why early graduation is unlikely.

"I think Andi teaches English One-oh-one," I said. "Or she used to teach it. So did her husband Sam before he was killed."

"She had a husband who was killed?"

I nodded. "Drunk driver. He taught at Edmund College. Her husband, I mean. The drunk driver was a student, but not at Edmund. Or NU either, I don't think."

"Wow. That's got to suck."

"They were only married for five years. Weird to think about it, because she totally loves David. Like, true love. It's so obvious. They got married this past New Year's Eve, precisely at midnight. But if Sam had lived, she and David probably wouldn't be together now. She said he was her true love too."

"That's pretty amazing," said Clark. "Some people don't even get one true love in their lifetime. Imagine getting two."

Was Lulu Lawrence true love? I wanted to ask. Couldn't have

been if she broke his heart. Or was that why hearts could be so easily broken—because true love could be broken too?

I can't imagine loving anyone other than you.

We continued to walk, and I wondered: Did we look like two people who belonged together? I hoped we did. I hoped we *were*.

"So how did the apartment search go?" I asked.

He focused his gaze on the scenery but still attended to me. "OK, I guess. Most places are September-to-May rentals because it's a college town, but I found a year-round place and put down a deposit for July."

My heart plunged to my feet. "You're moving in July? Why so early?" April was already almost over. *May, June... not much time.*

"I needed work too and figured I was better off getting something there as soon as possible, especially given how hard jobs are to come by."

"So did you get a job?"

He replied with a *mm-hmm*. "At the campus library. Working the circulation desk, maintaining computers, that kind of stuff."

"That's great," I said, and didn't even realize a tear slipped down my cheek until the drop touched my hand.

"What's wrong?" he asked.

I tried to keep the other tears at bay, but it was no use. I stopped in my tracks and covered my face with my hands, as if hiding them from him would make them disappear. "I'm sorry," I said with a muffled voice. "I just...I don't want you to go. You've become like, my best friend in such a short time. I know that probably makes me sound pathetic and you don't feel the same way, but—"

"How could you possibly think that?" he said, and drew close to me, enveloping me in an embrace. The smell of him was enough to make me want us to stand there for the rest of our lives. Like leather and a brand of cologne I didn't recognize. It was as if the world stood still for the two of us while we hugged. And even though he was inches taller than me, I fit so cozily against his torso, his biker jacket butter soft and acting like a solar collector. He let go, and I reluctantly let go as well. I searched to find sanctuary behind those Transition lenses; his irises the color of the sky, yet so serious and sad. I don't know how long we stayed like that, but the next thing I knew, his lips were touching mine.

Oh my God, I am kissing Clark Anderson. No, wait—Clark Anderson is kissing me.

I've kissed boys before, at parties during games—there were much more risqué versions that involved additional bases, drinking, and pot, but I'd wanted no part of that. My kissing experiences were nothing to write about, probably because none of them were with boys I liked beyond just a friend. And the one time Bottsy and I kissed was turned out too awkward to be nice, even though he said I was pretty decent at it. But kissing Clark in the middle of the rose gardens had to be the epitome of heaven. His lips were supple, not too wet, and he didn't slobber. My body felt like it had been lit on fire from the inside. I wrapped my arms around his neck and combed the ends of his hair with my fingertips as I kissed him more. I felt his hands touching the small of my back, one of them moving into the back pocket of my jeans, and the inner heat only intensified. *I could get addicted to this.* Like eating potato chips or something. Doctors would have to surgically unstick me from him.

Did he kiss Lulu Lawrence like this? Did she kiss better? *No, no, no—get out of my head, Lulu Lawrence! He's mine now.*

We stopped kissing for a moment, but remained in an embrace. Then we walked hand in hand to the gazebo, and kissed some more. "You're so pretty," he said softly. "You know that, don't you?"

I might have shaken my head no because he chuckled and said, "Well, you totally are." Then he put his forehead to mine, and I could feel his breath on me. "God, I so wish we'd met sooner." He paused for a beat. "If only you weren't a sophomore. If only you could come to college with me."

"I know," I said, willing myself not to start blubbering again. "If only my parents would let me transfer to another school. Or move in with David and Andi. I think they'd rather see a zombie apocalypse before that happened, though."

Clark's laugh sounded like a glorious melody.

"We'll find a way to make it work," he said. "We'll keep writing to each other, and be like those people who live on different continents and fall in love through letters for twenty years until they can finally be together."

Together—*together*! What a glorious word. But how? How does that work, when two people live so far away from each other? How can words on a page, or texting, or FaceTime possibly sustain anyone, especially when you know how it feels to be in someone's arms?

I didn't want finally, or eventually. I wanted *now*.

"Um, I don't think I can wait that long," I said with a nervous giggle. He kissed me again, each feeling more familiar than the next.

We stood in the gazebo and took in the panorama, Clark standing behind me with his arms in a protective lock, exactly the way David had stood behind Andi at my party when they watched me blow out the candles.

"Can I ask you something?" I said after a bout of dreamy silence.

"Shoot," he replied.

"Had you planned to go apartment hunting, or were you hoping to see me, knowing I was going to be in Northampton for the weekend?"

I turned around to get a glimpse of his face, and it revealed all. "Guilty," he grinned.

My insides went from feeling like they were on fire to

marshmallows. "I was hoping you'd say that. Now I'm even more mad at my parents for screwing up my plans."

"It's OK," he said. "There'll be other weekends. We have two months."

Two months. That's all. Was there a secret strategy for making two months stretch out to feel like two years? Was there a way to be in two places at once? Was there a way to actually convince my parents to let me live with David and Andi?

Clark looked down at his watch. "Although we'd better get going now. School's letting out."

Already time was slipping through my fingers. We held hands all the way back to Clark's car, saying little and smiling all the way. We continued to hold hands in the car, and he even leaned over to kiss me at a red light. When we finally pulled up to my house, he put the car in park and we kissed forever, breathing a little bit heavier, our mouths a little bit more open. Thank god my parents weren't home yet. We touched foreheads again. "Until tomorrow, Wylie Baker," said Clark in that same whisper as before.

"Until tomorrow, Clark Anderson," I repeated.

We kissed one more time.

"I don't want to leave," I said.

"I don't want to let you," he replied.

At that moment, Trish pulled into the driveway. *Busted.*

"Uh-oh. Now I have to go," I said, and opened the door. "Thank you for today—best day ever."

"I'm sure we can top it."

I couldn't wait to try.

Before I closed the door, I poked my head in one last time. "Hey, Clark? How come you ended up liking me and not my sister?" Or any other senior, for that matter.

He looked at me as if the question were absurd. "Why would I prefer her to you?" he asked.

"I don't know. I guess because you're in the same grade."

"She's not you," he said matter-of-factly. "None of them are."

Oh, yeah. Best. Day. Ever.

Chapter Thirteen
May

The sun shines a little bit brighter. Colors are more vivid. Food tastes better. Everything sounds like music. Things and people that normally irritate you slip by unnoticed. The most monotonous task gets done while smiling. Time passes differently, like you're more in the present moment.

So this was what it's like to be in love. Correction: This was what it's like when the one you're in love with loves you back. Granted, Clark hasn't said he's in love with me, nor have I said it to him, but given the recent events, I'd say we're both on the same page.

I'd confessed to Trish about cutting the rest of the school day with Clark after he left—I kind of had to, given that she'd caught me kissing him. She promised to keep my secret.

"Just make sure you either get on the pill or use condoms," said Trish.

"Ew!" I blurted back. "So not where I was going with this discussion."

"But you're going *there* with him, right?"

"Trish, we just *kissed* for the first time today. Plus he's moving up to Massachusetts in July. I don't know what's going to happen. At least he'll be living near David and Andi—how cool is that? I can visit all of them at once."

"Protect your heart" were Trish's last words before she'd changed her clothes and headed right back out the door for work.

Even though I wasn't a hundred percent sure if we were, I told my parents that Clark and I were dating now, asked them for permission for him to take me to and from school, and they consented. They wanted to meet him, though. So the first morning he picked me up, rather than honk the horn and wait in the car, he came to the door, rang the bell, and introduced himself to Mom.

"Hello, Mrs. Baker," he said, his tone a mix of I-have-the-utmost-respect-for-you and hey-how's-it-goin'. He extended his hand. "Clark Anderson."

My mom was her usual reserved self. "Hello, Clark."

"I really appreciate you allowing me to take Wylie to and from school. Oliver is very safe," he said, pointing to his car behind him. "Up to date on inspections and whatnot, and I'm an excellent driver. No tickets."

"Good to know," said Mom.

I kissed her on the cheek just as I was about to leave, and looked at her like, *Well?*

She replied with a look of her own: *OK, you have my blessing.* I could have squealed.

In addition to the car rides, we got to see each other at Study Hall—a.k.a. Heaven—for fifty minutes each day, where we still exchanged and read our letters. We put our desks together and held hands underneath them, and at the end of the day I'd find him leaning against my locker, waiting for me. After school he drove us to the deli to get snacks, and then we headed to Elizabeth Park. We listened to music, and not one of them a sappy love song. We made each other laugh and called each other by our last names or first and last names together and kissed and/or held each other every chance we could.

One night Mom came into my room while I was writing Clark a letter.

"I'm pretty sure that's not homework," she said.

"I'm on top of it, Mom," I snapped back.

"Are you sure? Because if you're not I'm going to insist that Trish start taking you to and from school again."

I looked up at her. "What? Why?"

Mom sat on my bed. "Wylie, I never pegged you as someone to revolve your entire life around one boy."

"I am *not* doing that!" I said. A little too emphatically, I realized. Shoot. "I just...I really like him, OK? He's my first real boyfriend. Don't ruin it for me."

"I'm not trying to ruin anything for you. But you haven't had any friends over since your party. Not even Roxanne."

A lump in my throat formed at the mere mention of Roxanne. I still hadn't told Mom what happened.

Mom continued, "You're not talking about the things you usually talk about. Even David and Andi seem to have taken a back seat."

Whoa. My mother and I have gotten into countless fights about how I'd supposedly neglected her and the rest of my family after I found David and started getting to know him. If she was sticking up for David and Andi, then maybe she was on to something.

"Mom, how do you handle it when someone you like likes you in a way that is more than the way you like them?"

Mom looked dizzy. "Say it again?"

I decided to come clean. "I found something out. About Bottsy. It turns out he likes me. Like, *like* likes me. And even though you know I love him, I don't, you know, I don't love him in that way."

Mom was as stunned as I had been when I first found out. "Wow," she said.

"I know."

"How did you find out?"

"Roxanne kind of blurted it out at lunch last week," I said. "In front of Bottsy." I sucked in a breath. "There's more. *Roxanne* likes Bottsy that way. So now, for some reason, she's all mad at me because I *don't* like him, and she's stopped speaking to me. And Bottsy hasn't spoken to me since that day either."

"He's probably embarrassed," said Mom. "I know I'd be mortified."

"What should I do?" I asked.

"Talk to them, I guess."

Why did parental advice always consist of talking to someone? Wasn't there another way?

"How can I talk to them when they don't want to talk to me? I've tried texting them a million times. They avoid me in the hallways. They won't even come to lunch period anymore." Tears came to my eyes. "You think my life is revolving around Clark? Well, I don't have anyone else right now."

Mom put her arm around me. "Wylie, that's not true. You invited lots of friends to your party. And you have all of us and…" I knew she couldn't bring herself to say David and Andi.

"People follow Christina, Mom. If she tells them I'm a loser, they believe it."

"As long as *you* don't believe it."

"Whatever," I muttered.

Mom stood up abruptly, and I knew I'd just blown it. But, like Mom, I was too stubborn to admit it. "Just keep on top of your homework, OK?" She left my room and closed the door behind her with a little more force than a calm person would, leaving me to glare at it as if she were still standing there.

Chapter Fourteen

I'd been looking forward to Skyping with Andi all week. Before we started in with the tutoring session, I told her all about me and Clark, including the letters.

"Funny, Sam and I used to write letters all the time. When we first met, I was still living in New York and he was living here. We emailed each other every day, way more than we talked on the phone. I think we were more comfortable with words on the page—it was more intimate, in a way. Not that we ever were in shortage of conversation when we saw each other in person…"

I couldn't imagine being so in love with someone and not seeing him every day. What on earth did people do before smartphones? I mean, obviously I know, but how did they get through it?

"Was it hard to have a long-distance relationship?" I asked.

"Actually, it was exactly what I needed at the time. I'd needed to ease into Sam. I wasn't very trusting, especially of my own feelings. I was terrified of being let down by a relationship again. Had we lived in the same state, I think I might have sabotaged it. But I quickly saw that Sam was different."

"How?" I asked, hanging off her every word. "How did you know?"

She paused to piece together her thought. "It's hard to explain. I felt at home with Sam, from the moment we met."

"You didn't feel that way with David?"

"David made me crazy," she said with a laugh. "He pushed all my insecurity buttons, and did so deliberately. But we'd become friends, and it was during those moments of friendship when I forgot to worry about how I looked or sounded or acted and was just myself. Otherwise every time I was around him my skin tingled, my pulse quickened, and I wanted to—um, kiss him."

"Ohmigod, that is *totally* how I feel about Clark! Everything you said—the feeling-like-yourself-when-you-talk and the skin-tingling and kissing thing." *Although why didn't I feel like myself the rest of the time, when I was in class or with my family?*

"Focus on the feeling-like-yourself thing," said Andi. "I think that's the most important. You know what my brother Tony used to tell me? 'Don't look for boyfriends; look for friends who are boys.' I wish I'd taken his advice early on. Would've saved me a lot of heartache."

I thought about Bottsy, and my heart flooded with memories: riding our bikes to the church parking lot when it was empty and having races; playing Twister and him making fun of me when my top fell over my head while I was practically upside down; having water-balloon fights. As we got older, we looked out for each other by swapping homework if we had the same teachers or giving each other a heads' up on pop quizzes. I decorated his textbook covers with custom artwork. He sent me playlists.

My heart sank. *Why did he have to like me? Why couldn't things have stayed the way they were?*

"I think maybe Clark felt the same way. He signed all his letters 'your friend'."

"That's really great, Wylie. I'm very happy for you. Will you tell David about him, or do you want me to tell him?"

"He'd probably want to hear it from me," I said. She agreed. "Do you think Clark is a dorky name?"

"My ex-fiancée's last name is Clark. No silent *e* at the end either."

"I still can't believe you were engaged to someone *before* you married Sam."

"It was a disaster, believe me," she said. "Or rather, it would've been had we gotten married. And a blessing that it didn't work out. Otherwise I probably would've been referring to him as my ex-husband."

"How does that happen?" I asked. "I mean, did you think he was the one? How do you really know?"

"I think you just *know*," said Andi. "It almost feels like every cell in your body tells you so. But you have to be careful, Wylie. Sometimes we want something—or someone—so badly that we'll fool ourselves into believing it's right, delude ourselves into thinking it's that 'knowing'. That's what I did when I was with my ex-fiancé. I think deep down I was afraid no one else was going to love me."

"What about David?" I asked.

"Sometimes something can be right, but it doesn't work out. People or circumstances or fears get in the way. David and I were right for each other, but not at the time we'd first met. For a long time he'd treated me like any other client. And I'd been too scared to tell him how I felt, so I'd given up on the possibility of us being together. It wasn't until I was with Sam that David confessed how he really felt about me."

Wait, what? A client? *What did she mean by that?*

"Oh," I said, distracted. But before I had a chance to ask her to clarify, she changed the subject. "So, let's talk English class. What have you decided regarding that extra-credit essay for 'Letter from Birmingham Jail'? I'd do it—after all, any chance you get to hone your writing skills is to your advantage. You might even be able to use it as a college admissions essay when the time comes."

Did she change the subject to deliberately throw me off course, or was she really oblivious to what she'd just said and was ready to move on? Either way, apparently we were done talking about Clark and David and love in general. I wasn't in the mood for a tutoring session.

"I have *no* clue what to write about," I said, forcing myself to press ahead. "I'm not even sure what it's about. I mean, I get that Martin Luther King was writing to the clergymen, and he was talking about why those marches were so important, but I don't understand why you wanted me to read it in the first place."

"One of the things that made King so powerful was his ability to persuade people to think and act differently. He did that both through his written and spoken words. And it's not just because of the words he used, but the way he used them. He embraced his readers— the clergymen—as co-thinkers, not enemies. He used powerful, personal examples to show what it feels like to be oppressed, and to persuade them of the immediate need for change. He referenced religious scholars and philosophers, demonstrating his own depth of knowledge and understanding."

I watched Andi on the screen as she spoke—she was so enthusiastic that her skin practically glowed. Meanwhile, I was trying to hide my boredom.

Andi continued. "I wanted to show you that if King could use language in such a way to create monumental change, then you can use language to create change in your everyday life circumstances."

Andi excused herself, walked away from the screen, and came back a couple of minutes later with a mug in her hand. She took a sip from it.

"OK," she said, gearing up, "I'm going to teach you about rhetorical appeals."

Uh-oh. She was in full professor mode.

I frowned at the unfamiliarity of the term. "What?" I said. "Sounds like Greek to me."

Andi chuckled. "It is. Good ol' Aristotle, in fact. I won't give you the Greek terms, but when Aristotle systematized a way of teaching oratory—giving speeches—he included these three approaches to persuasion. We use them in writing to this very day. What's confusing is that we teach these appeals or approaches as if we choose one and abandon the other two, but the truth is we use all three simultaneously, although one may be emphasized more than the others." She paused. "With me so far?"

"Can we go back to talking about Clark? I haven't even gotten around to telling you what happened with Roxanne."

"After this," said Andi. "The first appeal is to the moral character or credibility of the writer. What makes an audience trust a writer or speaker? For example, if David recommends you check out a particular artist, do you?"

Apparently I had no choice. I opened my notebook. "Most of the time, yeah."

"Why?"

"Because David knows a lot about art, and knows what kind of art or artists I like."

"So, you trust the source because of his knowledge and expertise not only of the subject of art, but also of you, his audience."

I quickly scribbled the example in my notebook. "I got it," I said. "Keep going."

Andi took another sip from her mug before continuing. "The second is an appeal to the emotion of the audience, be they readers, listeners, or viewers. Advertising and especially politicians love this appeal. For example, what kind of phone do you have?"

"An iPhone. My mom wanted to get me a Galaxy because she hates Apple products."

"Why?"

"She thinks they're all hype."

"So, she's not persuaded. Why did *you* want an iPhone?"

"Because, like, they were the first smartphone. They're cool, and they can quickly and easily do everything you would want to do."

"Would you have felt less cool not having one?"

"It's not that I'd feel less cool, it's that I'd feel like I was missing out on something."

"That's because Apple doesn't sell iPhones," said Andi. "They sell the *experience* of owning an iPhone. The belonging to the club, for example. Just like Amazon doesn't sell e-readers. They sell the e-reading experience. The appeal is not in the emotion of Apple or Amazon, but in the *consumer's* emotion." She paused again. "Still with me?"

I nodded. "I think so," although I wasn't one hundred percent sure. Then I added, "So this is what I'd learn in your class?"

She smiled. "Yep. Welcome to English One-oh-one—or, as it should be called, Rhetoric One-oh-one. Ready for the third appeal?"

"Go for it."

"OK, so the third is the appeal to logic, or reason—in other words, 'do it because it makes sense.' If you're making an argument, this is what you really want to emphasize. This, and your credibility, although sometimes the appeal to reason will amp up your credibility. Let's say you want to make an argument for extending your curfew—don't actually do this; your mother will kill me."

I laughed and crossed my heart. "I won't. Promise."

"Well, your credibility won't be as strong because you're sixteen and not a parent. And making an argument like 'all my friends can stay out later' isn't a reason. It's just a statement. Also, it's appealing to *your* emotion, not theirs. Their emotion is likely 'I-don't-want-to-worry-about-you-lying-somewhere-in-a-ditch'. So you have to appeal to common sense and collect *evidence* that supports a later curfew time as beneficial both to you and them. Take an actual survey of curfew times for sixteen-year-old males and females. Research social behaviors of kids with extended curfews as opposed to strict curfews, or even no curfews. And so on. And anticipate any objections they might have: safety issues, conformity issues, financial issues, et cetera."

Suddenly, it all clicked. "Ohmigod, Andi—do you think I could do this regarding my school situation? Like, put together an argument for switching to another school, or doing early graduation? I've even been thinking of doing something like getting a cosmetology license."

Andi seemed hesitant to respond.

"You can. But, Wylie, you have to be *thorough*. You can't just go looking for evidence that supports what you want. You have to find out your parents' reasons for not wanting you to go—that way you'll strengthen the appeal of your argument. You have to look at *everything*, even if it doesn't support your position, and you can't exclude it. The evidence might wind up convincing you to change your position before you have a chance to change anyone else's. And by the way, when I say *argument*, I don't mean an 'I'm-right, you're-wrong' fight. I mean a *conversation* in which your intent is not to be right, but to persuade your audience to think about your position in a way they hadn't before."

"God, why don't they teach us this stuff in high school?"

"Some do," she said. "In AP English classes, usually."

I made a mental note to ask Clark if he learned it.

"I mean, I really like my English teacher but I'd much rather be learning *this* than *The Grapes of Wrath*."

"Well, how about wowing your English teacher by turning your essay into a rhetorical analysis of 'Letter from Birmingham Jail' that focuses on the three appeals? I'll even send you a handout with the Greek terms—then you'll really knock his socks off."

I was now totally on board with doing that extra-credit work, plus begin an extra-curricular project of my own: I was going to persuade my parents to get me out of this god-forsaken school.

Chapter Fifteen

Clark and Wylie.
  Wylie and Clark.
  Wylie Anderson.
  Wylie Baker Anderson.
  Wylie Jean Baker Anderson.
  Mrs. Clark Anderson.
  Mr. and Mrs. Clark Anderson.
  Clark and Wylie Anderson.
  Wylie and Clark Anderson.

I came up with every possible combination you could think of, wrote pages and pages of signatures in my notebook. Tried to picture what it would be like to actually spend the rest of our lives together, to imagine him as an old man with white hair and wrinkles and a cane. I couldn't even picture my mom that way, much less myself. I thought about what Andi had said—was he *really* the one, or did I just desperately *want* him to be the one?

I couldn't imagine myself loving anyone other than him. I also couldn't imagine myself falling out of love with him. Couldn't imagine calling him my *ex*-boyfriend as casually as Andi referred to her ex-fiancé, like he was just some guy she knew and not someone she *almost married*. How did she feel about him now? I wondered. Did she hate his guts? Did she look at him and wonder what she'd been thinking? Did she ever wonder if she'd made a mistake by not marrying him? I couldn't bear to think of Clark that way. Couldn't bear the thought of uttering his name in contempt or even indifference.

Clark and I didn't cut any more classes, mainly because of my lecturing him about needing to graduate and get the hell out of West Hartford. And yet, I was in no hurry to see him go. But every day after school we drove to Elizabeth Park and walked through the rose gardens. It had become "our place," and I even found myself imagining that someday we'd get married there, wondering if outdoor weddings were permitted.

Trish thought it was weird that we went to the park every day and not someplace private where we could be alone.

"He hasn't even taken you to his room yet?" she asked.

"Why should he?" I replied.

Trish laughed, and it was one of those I'm-laughing-*at*-you-not-*with*-you laughs. "You're not really that naïve, are you? Guys will do anything they can to be alone with a girl," said Trish. "Especially guys his age."

"We *are* alone," I said. "I mean, we're in a public place, but we're by ourselves."

Trish looked at me like I just said something stupid. Which, apparently, I had. "I'm talking about *sex*. Why hasn't he made a move on you? Why haven't you made a move on him?"

"You told me I shouldn't have sex with him," I said.

"But you *want* to, don't you? I didn't think you'd actually listen to me."

"I guess I do," I said.

"Has *he* said anything about wanting to?"

I thought back to all of our letters and conversations. "Not specifically."

"Well, what have you two done?"

This was getting embarrassing. "I don't know. Mostly a lot of kissing and...touching, I guess."

"What are you and he touching?"

I stood up, arms raised in surrender. "OK, I am *not* talking about this anymore."

"Hey, do you want to have this conversation with Janine instead? Be my guest. Geez, Wylie, I never took you for a prude."

I put my hands on my hips. "I am *not* a prude. I just want to make sure it's right. That may sound foolish and naïve to you, but it's what I want."

"Wylie, everyone's first time sucks. It's awkward and painful and neither partner knows what they're doing and you're better off just getting it over with. Virginity is not some precious gift to be treasured. More like losing a tooth."

I didn't believe her. Or maybe I didn't want to believe her. I didn't go for all that Prince Charming fairytale stuff, but I wanted my first time to be *special*, and to be with someone special. I didn't want to "just get it over with." Trish didn't sleep around—I knew she was selective about who she was with. But her advice seemed contradictory—one minute she was telling me to stay away from Clark, and the next minute she was criticizing me for doing so. What the hell?

Damn Trish for planting the seed in my head. Another week passed, and I was increasingly bothered by the fact that Clark still hadn't invited me to his house after school, nor had we gone on any dates at night, although I knew he'd been helping his neighbor restore an old Dodge Charger he had his eye on if the GTO didn't work out. But I started to wonder if maybe there was another reason why he didn't want me at his house. Maybe he was lying about his family situation and he lived with a dad who was drunk all the time and a mother who worked six jobs. Maybe his mom was out of work and he was supporting her and his little brother. Maybe he was still in love and sleeping with Lulu Lawrence…

No. No, no, no. *Stop.*

Clark and I were sitting cross-legged in the gazebo when I handed him the letter I'd written last night. No way did I want him to read it during Study Hall. I'd been quiet and fidgety during both the car ride to the park and our walk.

"Can you read this right now please?" I asked, my hand shaking as I held the letter out to him. I'd even put it in an envelope.

Clark looked at me with concern. "Okaaay…" he said. I frenetically tapped my foot and tried to calm the nerves in my gut as I watched him carefully remove the letter from the envelope, unfold it, and read:

> *Dear Clark,*
>
> *I don't know how to talk to you about this without feeling like a total idiot, and I'm afraid to tell you how I feel. I know we haven't been dating for long (we are dating, right?),*

Clark chuckled and looked up at me. "Of course we're dating," he said. I smiled, thinking, *Yep. Feel like a total idiot.*

He continued reading.

> *—but I was wondering if you want to go all the way (this isn't necessarily an invitation), and if we're ready for that. If not, then I'm sorry for making an ass of myself. If yes, then maybe we should talk about it?*
>
> *Love, Wylie*

I had really struggled with whether to end with *Love,* given that we've not used that word yet other than things like, "I love the way you draw" or "I love how you make me laugh when I least expect you to." It was the first time I'd ever ended a letter to him as such. Even Clark stopped signing off with "Your friend"—now it was just "Clark."

He sucked in a breath, uncrossed his legs, stood up and leaned against the side of the gazebo. "Wow, Wylie."

Oh God. I totally screwed up, didn't I.

"Did I just ruin everything?" I asked, standing up as well.

"What? No, of course not. You were honest and respectful and you have every right to know where this relationship is and where it's going."

"So..." I said. "Where is it going?"

Clark stared at the horizon. "I'm not sure. I'm a little torn and confused. I really, *really* want to be with you, meaning I do want to go all the way with you. But..." Of course there was a *but.* He paused before returning his gaze to me. "...you're sixteen, and a virgin, and I don't want to hurt you."

"It always hurts the first time, doesn't it?" *Ohmigod, shut up, Baker!*

"Well, yeah, but that's not all I'm worried about. I'm talking about hurting you emotionally."

"How would you hurt me emotionally?"

"Girls get really attached once sex is in the equation." He quickly added, "Well, maybe that's a sweeping generalization. I suppose there are some guys who get attached and some girls who are detached." He paused for a moment. "I don't know what's going to happen to us once I move in July. We might make it, but we might not. And I know you don't want to hear this, but there is your age to consider."

I could feel my defenses going up. "What do you mean by that?"

"You're sixteen. I'm eighteen. You're not a kid by any means, but do you realize that if you and I had sex your parents could have me arrested for statutory rape? Even if it was consensual."

"That doesn't seem to stop anyone else," I protested. "Besides, how would my parents even know? Unless Trish ratted me out—which she wouldn't do given that *she's* had sex and they don't know, although who knows, maybe they do, and it wasn't when she was sixteen…" I rambled.

Clark took my hand. "Wylie, I want to. I really, *really* want to. Like, right now."

My heart thumped so loud and fast I was sure he could hear it.

"I do too," I said, and then I paused for a beat. "I mean, I do and I don't. I'm a little scared."

"What are you afraid of?"

"The hurting thing, for one. All my friends who have done it said it hurt the first time. There's also doing it all wrong, doing it and not liking it, or you not liking it—"

He interrupted me. "I'm sure that won't be a problem. And I would do my best not to hurt you that way."

We looked at each other so intently, and it was if someone lit a match to my feet, or a flare shooting up from my toes and out through the crown of my head. We took hold of each other and kissed, but I wanted even more. My breath quickened to loud panting as we kissed, and I slid my arms underneath his jacket, feeling for the ends of his T-shirt and slipping my hands underneath, his bare torso warming my fingers. I could feel him pressed against me. *Every part of him.* Clark stopped, put his forehead to mine like always, and breathed heavily. "Wylie," he uttered between hot breaths.

And then it happened. I *knew.*

It wasn't just about me daydreaming about weddings and dresses and flowers. It was about Clark and me being together, spending every day as more than friends, committing to each other for the rest of our lives, kids or no kids. I couldn't explain it, but it was as if the scene passed before me like a train, and I knew it like I knew my name and date of birth and ordinary things like that.

This couldn't be a delusion. It felt too real.

Was he feeling the same thing? Did he have that same moment of knowing, that lightning strike that felt more like a whisper of a breeze? Or was I just completely crazy? And what was I supposed to do with this knowing?

Start planning my life accordingly, I guess.

"Clark, I'm going to persuade my parents to let me graduate early and move in with David and Andi. Then I'm going to try to get into a school up there. Maybe Edmund College, or Northampton U, where Andi teaches."

"Whoa, hold, on, Wylie."

"Maybe there's even a cosmetology school I can go to."

Clark let go and looked at me with a bewildered expression. "Wylie, you don't just apply to any ol' college. Don't you want to go to Parsons or Pratt or someplace like that?"

"Who says I have to go to Parsons or Pratt?"

"I'm just saying, you have talent. You know you have talent. I don't think Edmund or NU has a fine-arts program."

"Who says I have to go into fine arts? Maybe I want to do something different, like cosmetology. Or maybe I'll find something else I like."

"Your life shouldn't revolve around me, Wylie."

I became annoyed with him. "That's not what I'm doing. I just figured…if you want to be with me, well, this is a way for us to be together, and then the age thing won't matter."

"Oh, like your biological dad will be just fine with you having sex."

"It's none of his business."

"It is if you want to live under his roof. Not to mention that you'll still be sixteen. Wylie, if you want to go to a different school to get a better education, then go for it. But if you're turning everyone's life upside down just so we can be together, well, that's a really big risk that might not pan out. Don't live your life for anyone else but you."

"Oh. My God. You sound just like my mother. Why does everyone think my going after something I want means I turn everyone's life upside down, like it's all my fault? Why don't I ever get to just go after the things *I want*, especially when it's a huge part of my life and my happiness?"

"Because the things you want aren't only about you. What about what *I* want, Wylie? I want you, but I also want a college experience. I want some independence."

"Do you or do you not want to be with me?"

Clark shook his head and huffed. "This is exactly what I was trying to explain to you at the very beginning of this conversation. I'm ambivalent. I don't want to turn your life upside down any more than I want you to turn mine upside down."

"Who says anyone's life is getting turned upside down? I just don't see that." I didn't like the look he was giving me. Like I was a little kid throwing a temper tantrum. "And don't you *dare* say I'm too young to understand."

Shit. Now he just looked plain mad.

Minutes of silence crawled by while I trembled on the inside, like an inverse earthquake.

Just when I thought he wasn't going to say another word, he spoke up. "I don't think you're ready to be in a sexual relationship."

I don't think you're ready to be in a sexual relationship. Every single word was a knife that stabbed me smack in the middle of my chest. And the one that cut deepest was *you.* He didn't say "you and I." He said *you. I* wasn't ready. At that moment I wished someone would hit me over the head and knock me unconscious. And erase my memory, while they were at it.

I couldn't stop the tears from rolling down my cheeks. Couldn't look him in the eye. It hurt even more because he wasn't taking my hand or caressing my cheek or doing or saying anything else to comfort me.

"I want to go home now," I said, staring at my sneakers.

"OK," he replied.

We walked back to the car, arms at our sides, and drove all the way back to my house in silence.

How? How was everything so clear one minute—that *knowing*—and then the next minute everything was falling apart and feeling like it was going to kill me any second? Maybe it wasn't "knowing". Maybe it was the delusion, just like Andi said. If only there was some kind of device that could detect one from the other.

When we pulled up to the house, Clark took my hand, and this time instead of that happy tingly feeling, it felt like a thousand pokes with a fork. "I'm really sorry, Wylie. This is exactly what I was afraid of."

"I am such a fool," I said, staring out the passenger window, unable to bring myself to look at him. "A total loser."

"You are *not* a loser," he said emphatically. "And you're not a fool either. You just haven't had any experience with this, and I have. Wylie, you have to keep dancing to the beat of your own drum. I recognized that quality in you the first day I met you. If you start trying to dance to mine or anyone else's, it just can't work. You've got to believe me. I tried to do the same thing with my ex-girlfriend, and she wouldn't have any part of it. I'm finally starting to see now that it was a good thing. She was at a point in her life when she needed to experience some things for herself. It wasn't that she didn't care about me. It couldn't work no matter how much she and I loved each other. And I don't feel about her the way I feel about you, Wylie. You're different. That's why I'm trying so hard to spare you."

Unable to hear anything past *she and I loved each other* (and did he say *loved* or *love*?), I didn't know whether to thank Lulu Lawrence or punch her in the mouth. Ditto for Clark.

"So... what now?" I asked.

"See you in Study Hall on Monday?" he asked. As if he didn't just break my heart.

"You don't want to see me this weekend?" I said.

"I've got to help my dad with a bunch of stuff around the house, remember?"

Funny, the last time he mentioned it he said he was going to try to get out of it, or at least take me out Saturday night. Just another excuse. He was probably never going to see me. Ever again.

"Fine," I said. "I have a ton of homework anyway," I lied. "Plus that extra credit essay."

"So I'll see you in Study Hall on Monday?" he repeated.

"Sure," I said. But I knew. He wouldn't be there. And he'd probably never come back—graduation or no graduation

Please, *please* let me be wrong about that one.

Chapter Sixteen

5:00: *Can we talk about what happened today?*

5:16: *I have a letter for you. Can I send it now rather than wait until Monday? Because something tells me you're not coming to SH.*

5:21: *So, are you ignoring my texts because of your stupid "let's write letters" rule, or are you genuinely mad at me, or are you being responsible and not texting while driving?*

5:54: *Clark, I acted like a jerk today. Please don't hate me.*

6:05: *No phones allowed at the dinner table, so if you try to text me and I don't respond, that's why.*

I refused to come downstairs for dinner. Mom came up to my room and tried to get me to talk about it, but I refused and laid on my tear-soaked pillow. Asked her to leave.

6:48: *Are you eating dinner?*

7:22: *Clark, please. Let's just talk about this, OK? No letters. No texting. Just call me. I'm not going to try to call you because I think the ball is in your court.*

8:06: *Voicemail? Really? You hate me that much?*

8:37 *Fine. Whatever.*

9:15: *Do me a favor and delete all my previous texts along with this one after you finish reading it. Pretend you never read them at all, if you haven't read them, because maybe you haven't. But if you have, then I'd understand if you testified at my insanity hearing.*

10:00: I'll just say goodnight. And I'm sorry. And I'm here if you want to talk.

At bedtime, Mom came back to my room. She stroked my hair and rubbed my back the way she used to do when I was a little girl. "I know it hurts now, Wylie. He's the first boy you've really liked, but trust me, he won't be the last."

"What if I don't want anyone else?"

"You will. I promise."

That was a promise I did not want kept.

"Did you ever cry over anyone like this?" I asked.

"Sure."

"Did you cry over David like this?"

She didn't answer right away. I studied her face as she went somewhere else in her mind. Watched the way her eyes darkened. Followed the contour of her cheekbones. Looked at the shape of her lips as they pursed with tension. "I was hurt, but not the way you are right now."

I sat up. "How did you know Dad was the right one for you?"

"I just decided he was," she said, replying in a way that implied she found the question to be odd.

"You didn't *know*? You didn't have a feeling?"

"He met every criteria for what I wanted in a husband. And he loved you as if you were his own. That was enough for me."

"What about *love*?" I asked.

"Well of course I loved him," she said. "I still do."

"But are you *in* love with him? Because I never see you holding hands or kissing in public or anything like that."

135

"Of course. We're just not that kind of couple," said Mom. "There's more to being in love than public displays of affection. It doesn't mean we love each other any less than couples who do. And it's different for couples that have been together for as long as Dad and I, as opposed to newlyweds. You get used to each other, and your relationship changes. Not better or worse, just different."

Maybe she did know I was thinking of David and Andi. Even though they've only been married since New Year's Eve, they'd known each other for, like, ten years or something like that. And even though Andi was once married to someone else, she and David still loved each other when they were apart. At least that's what they've told me on separate occasions. Andi said she loved both David and Sam in different ways, but at the time Sam was the one she wanted and needed to be with. But to see her and David now, it's so obvious that they're madly in love. If it was possible for them to finally be together after all those years and obstacles and other people, then why wasn't it possible for me? More to the point, if Clark felt the same way about me, then why couldn't it work out now?

Unless he didn't.

I missed Clark.

I missed Roxanne.

I missed Bottsy.

I missed David and Andi.

I was doomed to a life of loneliness.

Most of the night passed with me wide awake and staring at the darkened walls and ceiling. I was up by seven o'clock on Saturday morning, and did sit-ups to try to take my mind off Clark and the state of my life in general. By ten o'clock I knew I was never going to make it through the weekend with my sanity intact. I missed Clark fiercely, wanted to call him, message him, something, anything. But

I also knew that he wouldn't return them, and wouldn't be calling or texting me.

I knew where I wanted to go.

I knocked on Trish's door and she invited me in. I opened the door to find her sitting at her vanity, running a curling iron through the ends of her hair. "What's up, sis?"

"Do you have to work today?" I asked.

"Later," she replied.

"Will you drive me to Northampton? I want to stay with Andi and David this weekend."

"Did Dad and Janine say it's OK?"

I didn't answer right away, and she turned to face me as she released a curl. It bobbed and bounced into submission.

"I'll tell them I'm going to Roxanne's." Normally she would've been the one I would have called. We'd have bought pints of Häagen-Dazs and eaten out of the cartons, listened to music or watched movies via Netflix all weekend. Maybe if I told her I needed her, she'd come around. Maybe Bottsy stopped liking me, and we could all be friends again. Maybe I could persuade Bottsy to like Roxanne instead of me.

"What makes you think they'll believe you two made up? You'll be grounded for life if you get caught, not to mention what they'll do to *me*. And what makes you think Andi and David won't narc on you?"

"Maybe they will," I said. "I'll deal with it then."

She handed me the curling iron, and I finished doing her hair while she hemmed and hawed until I said, "I'll pay for gas."

"And for my silence?" she said.

"I recall you were all gung-ho the last time I snuck off to Northampton— and you didn't solicit bribes from me."

"That was different—you were on an adventure to find your biological father. Now you're just being annoying."

"Come on, Trish, please?"

"OK, fine. You pay for gas, and you are going to owe me big time."

"Deal," I said.

I threw a change of clothes and some essentials in a duffel bag and grabbed my backpack so Mom would think Roxanne and I would be studying. Trish was the better liar than me, so while I hid in the other room, she announced nonchalantly, "I'm going to the mall with Kayla. I'll drop Wylie off at Roxanne's, OK?"

I heard Mom say, "Wylie's going to Roxanne's?"

I called out, "Yeah, Mom, we made up and she invited me to hang out for the weekend. Please? We're just going to study and stuff."

I closed my eyes, crossed my fingers, and awaited her reply.

"OK. Call me tomorrow and let me know if you need a ride home."

My crossed fingers turned into an air-fist pump. "Thanks, Mom!" I called out.

I let Trish blast whatever music she wanted on route to Northampton while I stared out the window. All I could think about was Clark—wondering where he was, if he really was helping his dad this weekend, if maybe he was still in touch with Lulu Lawrence at this very moment. I'd been having these incessant revolving thoughts ever since yesterday. Same Clark-time, Same Clark-channel.

When Trish pulled up to David and Andi's new house around one o'clock, the driveway was empty.

"Um, you called to let them know you're coming, right?" she said.

"Will you lay off? Everything's cool," I snapped. I got out of the car, walked up to the garage, and poked my head through the window. One of their cars was inside. I turned and gave Trish a thumbs-up, and waved her off.

She powered down the passenger window. "You sure?" she leaned over and called out.

"Go!" I yelled, impatient. The window rose and she drove away. Then I walked to the door, rang the bell, and waited.

No answer.

Shit! The possibility that they went out *together* hadn't occurred to me. Stupid Wylie.

I texted Andi, then David: *Are you around?*

No response.

What to do? Should I sit outside and wait for them to return? It was a beautiful May day—sunny and cloudless and seventy degrees. But what if they were gone all day? Or for the weekend?

Just as I was about to call Trish and ask her to turn around and pick me up (if she answered her phone, that is—Mom and Dad constantly drilled her about not using her phone while driving), I remembered that David and Andi had hidden a spare key and told me about it. I wandered around to the back of the house and onto the newly built deck decorated with a patio table and chairs and a host of potted plants and trees. One of the pots contained an unobtrusive neon yellow dot painted on the rim—I never would have noticed had I not known to look for it. I stuck my finger in the soil on the same side as the dot, felt around (silently praying I wouldn't meet any worms) until it touched something smooth, took hold with my thumb and pointer finger, and pulled out the buried metal key. It easily slid into the back door keyhole, and I entered.

Wow. This was weird.

It wasn't like I was breaking in and entering, given that they'd told me about the key, and I wasn't intending to steal anything. Also, I was family. But they weren't expecting me, and I'd never been alone in their house before—their old one or this one, which was still so new you could smell the fresh paint and hardwood floors and carpet. Everything was unpacked, pristine, and looking like one of those model houses used as showrooms. The walls were painted in warm, cozy colors with complementary artwork and furniture in plush, yet livable fabrics. Strange, I kept forgetting they were rich. They never acted like it.

I dropped my bags by the entryway, cleaned off the key and left it on the kitchen table. Then I took a tour of the house, familiarizing myself with it and peeking into the bedroom designated just for me. They'd let me choose the color scheme and furniture; I went with dark eggplant for all four walls and the ceiling, a chandelier light fixture, zebra-print bedding with a ton of throw pillows in all kinds of colors, and modern furniture with clean lines—my room at home still had too many traces of girlhood: too much Barney purple, too many stuffed animals and jewelry boxes and too much clutter—although this one looked too neat and clean and sparse. It needed to be more personalized and lived in, like with photos and posters and stuff. A framed photo sat on the dresser: David, Andi, and me on their wedding day, moments before midnight on New Year's Eve, when they surprised everyone by announcing they were getting married right there on the spot. They'd told me in advance, as well as Andi's mom and brothers, and David's family. Andi's mom had sat off to the side for almost the entire party, except for the ceremony part. She had been nice despite Andi telling me how difficult their relationship had been all her life, especially when she was my age. My mother and I had our differences, but I couldn't imagine what it would be like to feel like she didn't love me. Sure, she didn't get me most of the time, but she clearly loved me. And Andi never said she didn't want her mother around; she said she didn't learn how to relate to her mother until the very end of her mother's life, and for that she was sorry.

I stared at the photo for a long time: David dressed in a designer suit and no tie; Andi in a Christmas-red, v-neck sweater dress and knee-high black leather boots, her face framed by layers of her chestnut hair, green eyes radiant; me in a plain black dress, my purple skunk stripe looking bold and rad.

Sometimes I thought I looked more like *their* daughter than I did my mother's. Was I awful to think that?

David and Andi's bedroom was at the end of the hall, and it oozed luxury, complete with reading chairs, a bay window with a nook to sit, and a ginormous, spa-like master bathroom that smelled like vanilla and flowers. If being in the house by myself wasn't weird enough, being in their bedroom was even weirder. I tiptoed around, inspecting every inch, as if trying to find a clue—to what, I don't know.

A car door slammed, and I ran out of the room and down the stairs. However, I didn't see anyone when I looked out the window. Looked in the garage too. Still no one.

I texted David: *Where are you?*

Five minutes passed. No reply. Then I texted Andi the same message. Still no reply.

I went downstairs and sat on the sofa in the living room. It practically molded to my body, like one of those memory foam mattresses. I'll bet they had one of those too. *What did sex on a memory-foam mattress feel like?* I suddenly wondered. Come to think of it, what did sex feel like anywhere?

The front door opened and I heard two people enter, chattering. I opened my eyes, disoriented. Then it all bombarded me: *Fugger-buggers, I fell asleep! What time is it?* It wasn't dark outside, but the sun was covered over with clouds. Should I call out *"In here!"*? Should I stand up? Should I text them and tell them to look in the living room?

David and Andi were in the foyer, in front of the stairs, and I peeked my head over the back of the sofa.

"You hungry?" she asked.

David took a step toward her. "Ravenous." His tone implied that he wasn't talking about actual food.

You could tell they were hot for one another—David was looking at Andi the way I look at anything chocolate. He gently backed her up towards the stairs, and then pinned on the risers. They were both laughing, until he started to kiss her neck as she slid off his jacket and unbuttoned his shirt.

Ohmigod, oh, my god—are they going to do it right there on the stairs in front of me??? How does that work, exactly? Ohmigod, I AM WATCHING MY FATHER AND HIS WIFE ABOUT TO HAVE SEX.

Andi moved her head to the right, exposing more of her bare neck for David's lips, a satisfied, lustful smile on her face, and then she gasped and sprang up, practically knocking David on his butt.

"Someone's in the house!" she yelped and pointed straight at me as I screeched, and David came rushing in, Andi behind him. They both stopped short as I put up my hands and screamed, "Don't shoot me!" even though neither of them had a gun.

"Holy shit, Wylie?" said David, catching his breath.

"It's me," I said, breathing just as loud and hard.

"What the fuck are you doing?" he yelled, his hand on his chest, shirt still mostly unbuttoned. I tried to look away. He'd never dropped the f-bomb in front of me before. I actually winced.

"You scared us half to death," said Andi, also trying to calm herself. "How did you get in?"

"With the key in the back," I said. "You said I could come over any time. I sent you both text messages. Didn't you get them?"

David looked at Andi. "We forgot to turn our phones back on." Then, to me, "We were at a…" He bent over to catch his breath again, the way runners do. "Shit, Wylie."

Ohmigod, what was I thinking, just showing up? I started to cry. Was sixteen the year of uncontrollable crying? Geez. "I'm sorry," I said. "I am so sorry."

David hastily buttoned his shirt and crossed the room to put his arms around me. "No, I'm sorry, Wylie. I didn't mean to get mad at you like that. You just scared us, that's all."

I held on to him and cried even harder. "What's wrong?" he asked as he consoled me. "Is everything OK at home?"

"Everything is awful!" I cried.

"What happened?"

I couldn't answer him. Andi left the room and came back moments later with a glass of water. "Here," she nudged gently. I let go of David and took the glass. "Drink it in sips," she instructed. I took a sip and calmed down. They motioned me to sit on the sofa, and flanked me on each side.

"Tell us what happened," said David.

"It's stupid," I said.

Andi figured it out in seconds, and gave me a knowing look that I've only seen on my mother and Trish. "Clark?" she said.

I nodded. "And Roxanne. And Bottsy. And Christina and Hillary and the whole school. Everyone hates me now." I could feel my face scrunch up again as I nodded and braced for the waterworks to return, but they didn't. Finally all cried out, I guess.

Andi put her hand on my shoulder, and from the corner of my eye I saw her communicate something to David by mouthing words. I buried my face in my hands and growled. "I am such an idiot!"

"Stop that," said David, with Andi saying simultaneously, "No, you're not."

"Do your parents know you're here?" Andi asked after a few seconds of silence.

I knew I had to tell them the truth. And I knew what their response would be. Why I'd thought they'd react differently, I don't know. I'd thought maybe they'd go along with my ruse of being at Roxanne's. Or even believe that my parents had given me permission, although they would've asked why my parents just dropped me off with no notice.

"They think I'm spending the weekend with Roxanne."

"How did you get here?" asked David, no doubt remembering the last time I showed up on their doorstep with no warning.

"Trish drove me."

"Wylie, you have got to stop lying to your parents like this, and you've got to stop making us complicit in your lies," scolded David.

Complicit. New word. I figured out its meaning by the context in which it was used.

"I'm sorry," I said, unintentionally sounding more annoyed than remorseful. "But I knew they'd say no, my mom especially, and I knew if I told you ahead of time, you'd make me ask them."

"We have to call your parents and tell them where you really are," said Andi.

"Fine," I said. "But please, *please* let me stay here. Tell them it's all my fault and I'll take whatever punishment they want to give me when I get back, but let me stay here overnight and take me home tomorrow. *Please!*" I begged, on the verge of tears yet again.

They leaned forward slightly and exchanged reluctant but decisive glances. "Only if your parents say it's OK," said Andi.

I threw my arms around her, practically knocking her over. "Oh, *thank you!*" I hugged David next.

David stood up, pulled out his cellphone, and looked at Andi. "I'll call Janine."

"Thanks, Dev," said Andi to David.

"Thank you," I echoed.

Chapter Seventeen

As usual, my mother was furious with me, although I couldn't blame her this time. She gave David an earful, then gave me an earful, then gave Andi an earful, then gave David another earful before she finally calmed down and he somehow persuaded her to let me stay for the night. Andi must have taught him those rhetorical appeals, because he certainly knew whom he was dealing with. I took my stuff up to my room while David and Andi made spaghetti and meatballs for dinner. They seemed to know not to press me, letting me eat without trying to force me into awkward conversation. Instead they chatted about the event they'd been to, some film festival or something.

I helped them with the dishes—it was the least I could do—and then asked to be excused to my room. It felt strange to say that—my *room*—although they seemed totally comfortable with it. About an hour later, I was sitting on the bed with the Kindle Paperwhite, trying to concentrate on one of the books Clark recommended, when I heard a knock at the door, and Andi entered with a plate of milk and cookies after I offered a "Come in."

She extended a plate of Mallomars. I took one and bit into it.

"Sorry I got you guys in trouble," I said.

"Your parents are upset, and they have every right to be. You jeopardized their trust, both in you and in us. That affects our ability to have a relationship with you."

"I'm sorry," I said yet again.

I expected her to continue to scold me. But after taking a sip of milk, she put the glass and plate on the table beside the bed and propped herself against the pillow, crossing her legs just like me. I sensed she wasn't doing it as one of those grownups trying to relate to teenagers as much as she just liked to sit that way.

"So Wylie, what's going on?"

I updated her on everything—first about Roxanne and Bottsy, and then about Clark and me and our conversation at the park. "I thought I knew, just like you said. But then it all fell apart so fast." Before she could say anything, I beat her to it: "Can I ask you a question?"

"Depends on the question," she said.

"How old were you when you…you know, went all the way?"

She froze. I probably should've told her she didn't have to answer the question, but I really wanted to know.

"Technically?" she said. I didn't know what she meant by that. I shrugged. She answered, "I was thirty-three."

I dropped my jaw. "*Seriously?*" I said louder than I'd intended. "Why did you wait so long? *How* did you wait so long?"

Andi shifted her position uncomfortably, only to go back to sitting cross-legged.

"Lots of reasons. Reasons I can't fully explain, and don't want to. Some of them were good reasons, and some weren't so good. But in the end it was worth the wait. I sometimes think if I had to do it all over again, I'd do it differently. But overall I think everything happened the way it was supposed to."

"David was your first, wasn't he." Something about this made me happy, especially when her face flushed as she looked down, letting her bangs fall over her eyes in an effort to hide it. "I knew it! No wonder you two are so in love."

"It was a long time ago," said Andi. "Then I married Sam."

"You obviously did it with Sam too, right? I mean, before you were married."

She looked like she was taken aback. "Of course we did," she said.

I stretched across the opposite end of the bed and propped my head on my elbow. "At the rate I'm going, I'll be lucky to do it at all."

"Look, Wylie, believe it or not, some women wait even longer. It's a very personal choice, and shouldn't be dictated by the norm. At least, that's the way I've come to feel about it."

"My sister told me to just get it over with."

"That's another way to look at it," she said. "It just wasn't the way for me." I didn't say anything. Just sat and stared at the wall. Andi was quiet too, biting into another Mallomar, until she asked, "Have you talked to your mother about this?"

I shook my head. "I can't. Ever since finding David, things have been so off with us. It's just easier to talk to you."

Andi seemed neither flattered nor satisfied with my reply. In fact, she looked like she was mentally deliberating on whether to continue talking to me at all.

"Have you tried to get back on track with her?" she asked.

"I don't even have the first clue how," I said. "I try, and then, I don't know, we just get mad at each other. There's no way I'm telling her I want to have sex with Clark. She'll think I'm not ready. But I am—I swear, I am."

Andi cocked her head to the side, as if trying to read me, and asked, "Do you want to have sex with Clark just to get it over with, or because you think you'll keep him if you do?"

"Neither," I replied. "I want to have sex with him because I love him."

"You haven't known him for very long."

"Don't most people, like, have sex on the first date?"

"Even if they do, it doesn't mean you should too."

I folded my arms in a sulky manner. "Well, it doesn't matter, because apparently Clark thinks I'm not ready for it either."

Andi paused for a second. "Well, you'll probably be mad at me for saying this, but I think he's right."

She might as well have punched me in the gut.

"What?" I said. "Why?"

"Because you're too conflicted about the situation. Because he's too conflicted about the situation. Because you tend to act first and consider the consequences later. When it comes to sex, that's not a good thing to do. It's not good in other situations either, but especially with sex."

"What, you think I'd do it without a condom or something? I'm not stupid, you know."

"I never said you were stupid, Wylie. But look at what you did today. You lied to your parents and showed up on our doorstep without any notice. You're keeping secrets from them. That's not something a responsible sixteen-year-old does."

"I texted you!" *Sure it was after the fact, but still...*

"*After* you arrived!" *Damn. She nailed me on it.* "What if David and I were going to be gone for more than an afternoon? What if you were alone in the house and there really was an intruder? What if there wasn't a spare key?"

"Don't you think I should have my own key given that I'm your daughter?" I caught myself immediately after saying the words. *Your* daughter. Not *"David's* daughter," like I usually say. My slip-up scared me. Did I mean you-plural, or you-singular? Had I really come to regard Andi as my mom? Did it mean I loved her more than my real mom? Did Andi even notice?

"That's a conversation for another time," said Andi. She certainly sounded like a mother at that moment. "The point is that even though you're sixteen now, you still have a lot to learn about responsibility. I'm not talking about things like doing all your chores or schoolwork. I'm talking about *personal* responsibility, the kind that takes others into consideration and involves an understanding of what's at stake when you make choices."

"I thought you *got* me," I said, hurt. "Clark said I dance to the beat of my own drum. That's who I am. That's who I *want* to be."

"Dancing to the beat of your own drum is great. It's terrific, actually. But that doesn't mean you disregard everyone else in the process. Ever see the movie *Dead Poets Society*?"

I shook my head.

She looked stunned. "Of course not. It came out when *I* was sixteen. Holy crap. OK. Well, you should. A lot of cute guys in that. Anyway, it's about an English teacher at a boys' prep school who encourages his students to think for themselves and embrace all life has to offer, but forgets to warn them of the consequences doing so brings. They're not always good consequences. Punishment, expulsion...even worse. *Every* choice we make comes with a set of consequences, be they positive, negative, or neutral. We have to be willing to accept them. And if we're not willing to accept them, then we don't make that choice."

I considered the consequences of my actions with dumping the can of Coke on Christina's head, sending all those text messages to Clark, not paying attention to what had been going on right under my nose with Roxanne and Bottsy. To say nothing of finding David and forging a relationship with him and Andi while my parents were forced to watch. I further considered the consequences of successfully persuading my parents to let me transfer to a new school, or *not* sleeping with Clark.

"Do you think sixteen is a good age to have sex?" I asked.

Andi looked pensive, as if deliberating on whether she should respond. "No, I don't," she finally said. My heart sank. "People will probably tell you that's a prudish answer. And maybe it is. Maybe I am a prude."

"I don't think you're a prude," I said, jumping to her defense as if someone other than herself had actually just accused her of this.

Andi smiled in gratitude. "I don't think you need to wait as long as I did, but I think you need to at least be out of high school and get to know someone really well. I'm sure plenty of people would disagree with me and think I was some kind of freak for waiting as long as I did."

"Do *you* think you were a freak?"

"I used to. Not anymore. I don't know, it was inexplicably the right time for me."

"Were you and David in love when you and he had sex for the first time?"

"I think so," she said. "It was a very emotional time. His dad had just died and…" she trailed off. "I probably shouldn't be telling you this. I don't think he'd want you to know."

"But I *do* want to know," I pleaded. "I mean, I don't need details, but I want to know *him*. I want to understand."

Understand what? Even I didn't know what I was talking about.

"We broke up very soon after that," said Andi. "I had made the decision to move here and be with Sam. I knew what the consequences of that would be. I was going to hurt someone I loved and possibly give something up just as it was beginning. There was no guarantee that things would work out with Sam. All I knew at the time was that Devin was in no emotional space to be in a relationship, and Sam was already all in. I needed that all-in."

My ears perked up. "Devin?"

She reflexively put her hand to her mouth. "I'm sorry. I meant David."

"But you had sex with him when he was Devin?"

"Yes," she said. "I knew him as both."

I knew she had known him when he went by Devin. "Why did he change his name?" I asked yet again.

"Because David is his real name," she said. "It's who he really his."

"No, I mean why change it to Devin in the first place? And why did you refer to yourself as 'a client' that night during our Skype session?" I put up my hand before she even opened her mouth—I could already see her reluctance. "I know, I know... you're not going to tell me. Whatever."

"Wylie..." Andi started, frustrated.

"Just tell me he wasn't an axe murderer or something."

"Nothing like that. Listen, Wylie," I knew she was about to change the subject. "Based on everything you've told me, I can tell that Clark cares about you very much. If he didn't, he wouldn't be telling you that you weren't ready for sex. And if he's confused and needs time to work things out, then have faith that they'll work out in a way that's best for everyone."

"But what if that means we break up completely? I can't picture feeling about anyone the way I feel about him."

"Believe me, I've been there. You don't always get what you want. Life is just downright unfair sometimes. But it's the choice you make *in response* to whatever life gives you that matters. And you always have that freedom to choose the response. No one can take that away from you. You can choose to be miserable, or that you're never going to love anyone the way you love Clark and thus will spend the rest of your life single. Or you can choose to find happiness in spite of losing the guy you loved so much."

"Like you did," I said.

She nodded. "Like I did."

My head was spinning. I couldn't picture Andi in any kind of troubled state—even now, a mere two months since her mother's death, she seemed so in control. Maybe I too could dare to envision a life without Clark, or with someone other than Clark.

"Thanks, Andi. For everything." I leaned over and hugged her.

She gave me a squeeze and smiled warmly when we let go. "You're welcome." Then she picked up the glass and plate and went to the door. "Maybe we can work on that extra-credit essay tomorrow."

I smiled. "Sure thing."

I'd expected David to come in next to give me his own pep talk, but he never showed up. Honestly, it bothered me. David was so eager to be a dad to me that sometimes he came on a little strong. Maybe the pendulum was swinging the other way and he was trying to give me some space?

I stayed in my room and wrote letters to Roxanne and Bottsy. Rehashed the last couple of days. Filled them in the way I would if we were face to face. Told them I missed them. Told them I was sorry. Begged them to talk to me. (Lately I'd been begging everyone to talk to me. When did I become so pathetic?) I didn't know if I would actually send them, but it at least passed the time and was the next best thing to actually talking to them. Around ten o'clock I padded down the hall to say goodnight to David and Andi, when I heard them arguing. I crept closer to the door and leaned in to listen.

"She has a right to know, Dev," said Andi.

"How many times have we been over this?" said David. "Janine and Peter don't want her to know, and *I* don't want her to know. And it's not your call."

"You all think you're protecting her, but the truth is you're protecting yourselves. And when she finally does find out she's going to resent you—*all* of us—for not telling her. Hell, she already does."

"Exactly what I'm afraid of—her resenting us, but not because we kept it from her."

"She's sixteen years old," said Andi. "I think she can handle it."

I wasn't old enough for sex, but I was old enough to handle my father's past? That was encouraging.

"Could you have handled knowing something like that about your father at sixteen?" said David.

Whoa. Maybe I didn't want to know.

"When I was sixteen I would've loved to know anything about my father," said Andi. "Especially something that explained why he treated me the way he did. Dev, it's part of her life story. She's at an age where she's starting to make decisions about the rest of her life and who she wants to be. How can she do that if she doesn't know the whole story?"

I wanted to barge in there and say *YES! PLEASE tell me!*

The room went silent. Then I could barely hear David say, "I don't want to lose her."

"You may for a little while," said Andi, just as softly. "But not for long."

"Even a little while is too long," he replied. He then spoke even softer, and this time I couldn't make out the words.

I crept back to my room and went to bed without saying goodnight to them. Whatever secret they were keeping, I vowed not to hate him for it. I lost Roxanne and Bottsy. I was losing Clark, if I hadn't already. I was holding on to my parents by a thread. I didn't want to lose my father too. If only there was a way I could convince him of that.

Chapter Eighteen

The following morning, Sunday, Andi and I discussed "Letter From Birmingham Jail" and made an outline for what she called a "rhetorical analysis" while David was in his office. I wondered if they were deliberately staying apart because of the fight they had. I couldn't even ask Andi because then she'd know I'd been eavesdropping. After lunch, David offered to take me home.

Andi stood at the doorway and said goodbye to me.

"You're not coming along?" I asked.

"I've hogged enough of your time," she said.

I hugged and thanked her again. Then David leaned in and planted a goodbye kiss on her lips, and once again I saw them talk to each other without words. Whatever bad feelings they'd had seemed to have disappeared. My God, how I wanted to do that with someone one day, especially with Clark.

"Love you," he called to her as we stepped outside.

"Love you," she echoed, and stood in the doorway, waiting for us to leave, waving.

As we pulled away from the house, David said, "Andi said you two had a good talk last night."

What, specifically, did she tell him? I wondered, other than what I'd overheard. Did she tell him we were talking about them having sex? Did she tell him about my wanting to have sex with Clark?

I simply nodded. "Mm-hm."

"I know you can talk to her about things you can't talk to me about. I'm glad you trust her so much."

"She gets me," I said. "I think you get me too, but…" I stopped, not knowing how to finish my thought.

"But I've not been willing to share some things about myself," he said.

Ohmigod, was he FINALLY going to tell me? Had Andi actually persuaded him last night?

"You know I used to go by a different name," he said.

"Devin," I replied.

He practically cringed when I said it. "Yes, Devin."

"It's where Andi got the name *Dev*. Because she knew you first as Devin."

"Yes," he said, "and it's the only thing from my past life that's stuck. The nickname was endearing, something that bonded us, in a way. She's the only one who ever called me that, before or since, and the only one I'll ever allow. But sometimes the name is also a reminder of a life I no longer want anything to do with."

"Whatever it is, I'm not going to hate you," I said. *An emotional appeal?* "I know you're afraid of that, and you don't have to be. Unless you, like, killed someone."

"I didn't kill anyone," he said with a crooked smile as he merged onto the highway.

He drove for about a mile or two before resuming conversation. "I didn't have a great relationship with my father," he started. "A lot of Andi's problems with her mother were parallel to my experiences with my father. And both of our parents met the same fate, unfortunately."

"Did you make up with your dad the way Andi made up with her mom?"

"Yes and no. We came to an understanding." He looked sad. "Anyway, he never approved of my love for art. Thought it was gay." He said the word in a condescending way, as if he was impersonating his father, and I knew it wasn't a mentality he himself advocated.

David continued. "This will probably sound like a bunch of pop psychology, but some part of me wanted to prove to my father that I was a man. And it led me to do some things that were morally questionable."

He paused again; I was hanging on every word.

"I spoke to your mother earlier, while you and Andi were working on your essay. I think it's time for you to know some things. Your parents and I didn't want to tell you for a number of reasons, but I'm now convinced that not telling you will be even worse."

"So, you're finally going to tell me now?" I said, practically chomping at the bit.

"Your parents and I will sit down with you later this week."

You know that sound a balloon makes when the air goes out of it? How it looks? Yeah, that was me just then. Like someone put a big present in front of you, said it was for you, then told you you weren't allowed to open it until they said so. But you had to just sit there and look at it. *Ugh.*

"OK. Thanks," was all I could say.

"Thank my wife," he said. I could tell he liked calling Andi that, especially since he'd never been married before. "She's the one who convinced me, which helped me convince your mom." I bet he didn't tell my mom that part.

"Andi knows a lot about the art of persuasion," I said.

He smiled with equal parts pride and affection. "Yes, she does."

David drove for a long time with neither of us speaking, but it didn't feel like an awkward silence. At least, not until I was aware of the fact that so much time had passed. I looked at him, staring straight ahead at the road, lost in contemplation. He looked so much like me—the color and shape of his eyes (*sienna*, according to Andi, and she was right), the way he looked so fixedly at something, with a fierce determination… it was both comforting and freaky.

"David?" I said.

"Yes?"

"Maybe I should call you something else."

"Like what?"

"I don't know. My dad is Dad. I can't stop calling him that, nor do I want to."

"Nor should you," David added.

"I want to call you something like Dad too, but it's too confusing."

"I understand," he said. "Maybe there's something else, something that no one else says?"

"Kind of like the way only Andi calls you Dev."

"Exactly," he said. We both racked our brains, and he chortled. "I suppose *Father* is out of the question."

"Um, yeah."

He mimicked a snobbish voice saying, "Hello, *Father*," and we both laughed.

"What about 'Pop'?" I suggested.

I watched him mentally try it on for size. He wasn't convinced.

"Or I could just shorten it to 'D'," I offered. "Or is that stupid? I don't know. I was thinking D for Dad, D for David…"

"D for Dev…" he said.

This one had potential.

"Should we try it out for a while?" I said.

He turned to me for a second and cracked a grin. "Sure." After a beat, he added, "Shall I have a name for you as well?"

"I would really like that."

He paused to think. "I call Andi *cara*—it's an Italian word meaning 'dearest.' Perhaps I can call you *carina*. It's an offspring of that."

"Ooh, I like that," I said. "I especially like the way you say it."

"*Carina* it is."

"Thanks, D," I said, and chuckled. It sounded silly, yet fun.

He laughed heartily, took my hand, and gave it a squeeze before letting go. "I love you, Wylie," he said quietly, almost to himself, still looking at the road ahead.

"I love you too, Father," I replied. His eyes teared up.

Chapter Nineteen

When we arrived at my house, David walked me to the door and I invited him in. He stepped into the foyer, where Mom met us, Dad following behind her.

"You, go up to your room," said Mom to me.

"Geez, not even a hello?"

"Upstairs. I'm still furious with you."

I turned to David, about to give him a quick hug, but something stopped me: *What would be the consequences of hugging David in front of my parents, especially when they were so upset with me?*

Instead, I just smiled. "Thanks for letting me stay over," I said.

"You're welcome, *carina*," he replied, and winked. I couldn't help it. I liked the new term of endearment, and I knew it showed on my face. I also knew my parents both saw the exchange. "See you in a few days."

I charged up the stairs, and sat inconspicuously on the top riser to listen in on the conversation below.

"Thanks for bringing her home," said Dad.

"You're welcome," said David. "Thank you both for agreeing to talk to her with me."

"I'm still not convinced this is a good idea," said Mom. "Especially after what just happened. What if she runs away again? Where will she go this time?"

Oh, please don't cave, David!

"I think she learned her lesson. There's no good reason to postpone the inevitable, and if we're discussing it as a family, I don't think she'll run off anywhere, especially not if we all rally around her in support."

I quietly exhaled a sigh of relief.

"This is going to be the most awkward conversation I've ever had with anyone," said Mom.

Ew. That can't be good.

"I'll do all the talking, if you want," said David.

"You'd damn well better," said Mom, "given that you're the one that got us into this mess."

I could hear David make a huffing sound. "Janine, honest to God, I don't get your attitude, and I don't get your point of view. We don't have a 'mess.' We have a *daughter.* I know I treated you like shit sixteen-plus years ago, and I've been contrite ever since. Can you maybe let me off the hook, especially since you didn't even give me the courtesy of letting me know we have a child?"

I charged back down the stairs. "Don't you talk to her like that! You know that's not what she meant. What about letting *her* off the hook?"

David looked at me, flabbergasted. So did my parents. Even I couldn't believe what I was saying. For the first time ever since finding out about David, I was sticking up for my mom rather than blaming her.

"You need to leave now," said Dad to David. Most of the time my dad was quiet and withdrawn, but even a hint of a cross eye aimed at one of his family and he would take off the gloves and fight to the death. Didn't matter that David had a couple of inches on him in height and worked out regularly at the gym. (Hello, Confrontation? Peter Baker, here. I am not afraid of you.)

David relented. "I'll see you in a few days," he said, and then left.

Mom turned to me. "Go back up to your room." *Didn't she even care that I just defended her?*

As I made the slow climb back up the stairs, I heard Dad say, "He's right, you know. You've got to let it go, and not just for Wylie's sake."

Then I heard my mom say, "She's a reminder, Peter."

"Of what?" he asked, sounding angry. "Of who you really wanted?"

Was that true? Was David who she'd wanted all along? Had she settled for my dad all this time? Was I nothing but a reminder of someone who didn't want her? Was that why I sometimes felt like she didn't want me? Was that why she didn't like Andi?

It was my fault. It was all my fault. If she'd never had me, then none of this would have happened. I made her entire life miserable.

The front door slammed just as I reached my room. I closed my bedroom door, sat on the edge of the bed, and shook. Five minutes later, Mom entered my room without knocking. Her eyes were puffy.

"Wylie, Dad and I are very upset with you for sneaking out and involving your sister yet again."

Either she didn't know I'd heard what Dad said to her, or she did and was pretending otherwise. Either way, I had to play along.

"For the record, she didn't go willingly," I said in defense of Trish. "I really had to twist her arm to do it. You shouldn't punish her."

"Do you understand that not telling us is the problem?"

"Yes, I do," I said. "But had I asked, would you have let me go? After all, you changed my plans with David and Andi without even giving me a say."

"I don't understand why you had to go there in the first place."

"Because I needed to get away. I was upset about Clark and Roxanne and Bottsy—I lied to you, Mom. We haven't made up—and I wanted to go someplace that made me feel good about myself."

My mother seemed taken aback, and I thought for sure she was about to tack on lying to the list of my punishable offenses. "You don't feel good about yourself here?"

I couldn't keep it in for another second. "Is it true?"

"Is what true?"

"Did you really want David?"

She sighed in exasperation, "Wylie..."

"I'm sorry, Mom. I'm sorry for being a constant reminder. I'm sorry for looking like him. I don't know why you had me if it hurts you this much."

Mom began to cry, "Stop it! I didn't mean it like that. I have *never* regretted having you. How can you even think I would have been better off? You are the best thing that ever happened to me. You are the love of my life, Wylie Jean—don't you know that by now? I would do it all over again in a heartbeat as long as it meant having you."

I plowed into her arms, and we both stood there and cried for a long time.

"I should have told him. I should have told him and you from the very beginning. *That* was the mistake I made—not *you*. That's the reminder. I know I've blamed you for wanting to find your father and then having a relationship with him. But the truth is, I blame me. I was selfish. I wanted you all to myself. I still do. And every time I see you with him, I'm afraid I'm going to lose you to him. Every single time. I can't seem to let it go." She began to cry again.

"You're *never* going to lose me. Why can't you believe me?"

"You're right," she said. "I need to trust you more. I need to believe you. I'm sorry I made it so that you have to sneak around to see him. You shouldn't have to do that."

"I never should have snuck around last year when I went to find him. I should have told you what I was doing, just like I should have told you the truth yesterday. I didn't stop to consider the consequences of my actions."

We stopped hugging and I pulled back to get a good look at her mascara smudged under her eyes like watercolor, tear streaks cutting vertical paths through her blush, lipstick cracked and faded.

"You need a makeover," I said.

She dabbed under her eyes with her fingertips.

"Gee, thanks, kid."

"No, I didn't mean it in a mean way. I meant that I want to do your hair and makeup right now." Mom looked in the mirror. "Come on, it'll be fun!" I said as I pulled my desk chair to the middle of the room and practically pushed her into it. She gave in. First I removed her makeup with some disposable cleansing cloths. Next I pulled out trays of foundation, shadows, and blushes from my top drawer.

Mom's eyes nearly popped out of their sockets. "Holy… what did you do, knock over a cosmetics counter? Where did you get all this makeup, Wylie?"

"This is where most of my allowance goes now. And hair products too. I guess I'm a little obsessed."

"A little." She fixed her focal point on a painting hanging on the wall that I'd done last summer. "What about your artwork and drawing and painting? Don't you love that anymore?"

"Sure I do. In fact, that's what doing makeup feels like. It feels like painting. And doing hair feels like sculpting with clay or something like that."

"I had no idea."

I applied a new foundation on her that was much lighter in consistency and more aligned with her skin tone, followed by a brushing of mineral power to seal it. Next, I chose a violet shadow—if applied too heavily, it would look loud and gaudy. But paired with a neutral shade and used on the crease rather than the lid, it brought out the color of her irises. Next, I ditched her usual black mascara in favor of brown, and applied it only on the top lashes. I also opted for a pencil liner rather than liquid, and worked a subtle line around the outer corners rather than across the top and bottom lids.

"So, how was it at David and Andi's?" Mom asked.

I was startled by the question. "It was OK. They weren't too happy about the surprise visit either. I guess it really was a dumb move on my part."

"Do you feel better about things?"

"A little. I still have no clue what to do about any of it, though. I mean, no one's speaking to me now."

"Wylie, I've never known you to be held back by obstacles. When you want something, you go for it. If you want Roxanne and Bottsy back, go get them. Same with Clark."

"How? And what if they don't want me?"

"Then they weren't really your friends."

"That is such a parental thing to say."

"It's the truth, though. And I can't believe that after all these years your two best friends would dump you for something so petty. And if they do, trust me, they'll both regret it years from now."

"How can love be petty?" I asked.

She didn't respond.

The blush was next—should I go with pink, or bronze? I tried a shade in between, also from the minerals collection. Despite not being fully convinced that I'd chosen the right color, I applied it with a fat, fluffy brush over her cheekbones—the key word was *subtle*—and sure enough, less was more. The shape of her face completely changed, giving her definition and contour.

"Ohmigod, wait until you see this! It looks *so* fabulous!" I squealed.

"I trust you," she said, although everything about her tone and the look on her eyes spoke to the contrary.

I chuckled. "You should."

Finally, the lips. First I used a lipliner pencil, which magically transformed her mouth from horizontal and straight to round and puckered. Then I found a gloss that was neither too neutral nor too pink, and used a thin brush to apply it.

"Can I see it now?" she asked.

"No—I still have to do your hair."

She groaned. I ignored her and pulled out my blow dryer and a round brush and completely re-styled her hair, changing the part from the middle to the side, and curling the ends outward rather than underneath, like a flip.

"You should change the color too—something a little less stark. I think you need neutrals, Mom. You're still stuck in the eighties when loud was a good thing."

She chortled. "I thought you liked all those eighties looks."

"Some of them were cool. But on a woman of your age…"

"You're a barrel of compliments today, kiddo."

I polished her off with a texturizing cream, did a quick spray around her head with a finisher, and stepped back to get a full view, like taking in a finished painting.

I dropped my jaw in amazement. "Oh. My God. *Look*."

Mom stood up, tentatively approached the mirror, and her reaction was as if she had never seen herself before.

"Wylie," she said more like a breath.

"You look so beautiful, Mom. You *are* beautiful."

She couldn't stop staring at herself. "You were right. It looks fabulous." She turned to me and smiled wider than I'd seen her smile in ages. "Thank you," she said. She then looked at the mess of open tubes and compacts and jars. "Do you want to do this for a living?"

"I'm thinking about it," I said. "There's even a program you can do while you're still in high school."

She seemed to consider the idea. "You're extremely talented."

I beamed. "Thanks, Mom."

Just then, Dad entered after a quick knock. He was about to speak, but did a double-take when he saw Mom, and gaped at her the same way she'd just gaped at herself in the mirror.

"What do you think?" I asked. Mom seemed just as eager as I was for his response.

He just stood there, totally mesmerized. Mom's happy smile softened.

They gazed at each other the way David and Andi do.

"I'm sorry about before," said Dad to Mom. He sounded so tender, so remorseful.

"It's OK," she said gently. "So am I."

It was like they forgot I was in the room. I was about to wave a hand between them when Dad snapped out of it.

"You two get everything squared away?" he asked me.

"We're good," I said. "I'm really, *really* sorry for sneaking off and not asking for permission. It was very stupid of me and I won't do it again, promise."

"OK," he said. And then, he took my mother's hand and led her to the door. *He took her hand!*

They were about to head down the hallway when Mom stopped and said, "Oh, and you're grounded until the end of the school year. No going out after school, no TV or computer other than homework from eight to bedtime, and no phone on the weekends. And your visiting David and Andi in Northampton again? Not happening anytime soon."

Put a lock on my door and bars on the windows, while you're at it.

"OK," I said as she closed the door behind her.

I was willing to take the consequences of my actions. I was willing to be responsible.

Chapter Twenty

The weekend had passed so slowly that my confrontation with Clark felt like it had happened longer than mere days ago. I dreaded going to school on Monday morning, but Trish reminded me to dress to impress.

"Don't put your hair in a ponytail. Wear makeup. Wear sexy underwear. Wear your best outfit."

So I did just that: got up extra early to wash my hair and blow it out silky sleek; applied makeup casual chic; wore matching underwear from Victoria Secret's *PINK* collection; and topped it with skinny jeans, leopard-print baby doll top, and royal blue ballet flats.

I looked good, if I do say so myself. Trish agreed.

"Knock 'em dead, Sis," she said with a smile. Thankfully Mom and Dad didn't punish her for driving me to Massachusetts.

I found Roxanne eating lunch by herself at our usual table and, with butterflies flapping away—no, not butterflies; more like bats—I gripped my lunch tray and approached the table like a girl on a mission.

"Hey Rox," I said, hoping a no-big-deal-attitude would break the ice with her.

It didn't. Roxanne looked up at me with an icy glare. "Hey."

Undeterred, I pulled out the chair opposite her and sat. "So I did a totally stupid thing this weekend. I made Trish drive me to David and Andi's without telling my parents *or* David and Andi, and they all flipped out. I'm like, pretty much grounded for life now."

She was completely uninterested. "Is that my top?"

I frowned. "No, it's mine." I couldn't take it anymore. "Look, Rox, I'm sorry, OK? I'm sorry I wasn't paying attention. I'm sorry I didn't know you liked Bottsy. And I can't help that Bottsy likes me—I didn't even *know* he likes me. I don't understand why you're so mad at me, but I hate it." Tears welled in my eyes. "I miss you guys so much. I so needed you this weekend."

"It's not just the whole Bottsy thing. It's *you*. First your father, now Clark Anderson. It's like we've become total afterthoughts to you."

Could that have really been true?

"How can you say that? You're the only ones I trusted to know about David." I was about to further defend myself when I remembered what my mother had said about wanting me all to herself. Roxanne was an only child. Maybe she'd wanted me all to herself too. And Bottsy. And with all my complaining about wanting to leave school, leave West Hartford, maybe she thought she was losing me.

Guilt and remorse consumed my entire body. "I'm sorry, Roxanne. I really, really am. I'll do better. I promise, I'll do better. I just want us to be friends again, OK? Please? Can we try?"

She wouldn't even look at me.

"Where is Bottsy, anyway?"

"He goes to the library during lunch now. He's avoided me ever since I made an ass of myself."

"You did not make an ass of yourself," I said. "And if it's of any comfort, he's been avoiding me too."

She looked up and away at nothing in particular, her eyes watery. "I don't know how it even happened," she said. "One minute he was just Bottsy, and the next minute he was more. If I could take a pill and make the feeling go away, I would."

"Or give him a pill to make him feel that way about you," I offered.

She attempted to smile. "It was just so much better the other way. It's like I cry all the time now."

"Ohmigod, *me too*," I said. "Ever since I met Clark, it's like I'm an emotional yo-yo. And Friday *I* made a total ass of myself. He probably hates me now."

"I doubt it," she said. "Everyone likes you."

"Except Christina and her lackeys," I reminded her.

"Christina is so freaking jealous of you she can't see straight. She wants everything you have. She always did. I'm not talking stuff, I mean like how thin and pretty you are and how easily you talk to people and are never afraid to say what's on your mind. It's like you're popular without even trying, and she has to work for every inch of space she gets."

I'd never seen it that way before. It explained why Christina went after me with such a vengeance. I'd cut her down in front of everyone at my party. She couldn't just get back at me. She had to destroy me.

Roxanne paused. "Kind of like me."

I gave her a startled look. "You... you're jealous of *me*?"

She sheepishly averted her eyes. "Well, I was."

"Rox, you are *so* pretty. And smart. You're way smarter than me."

"Fat lot of good it does me."

"Think about it. You'll be able to go to any college you want. You can be, like, an actual rocket scientist."

Roxanne laughed, which was exactly what I was hoping for.

"And you're not Witchy McBroomstick like Christina."

Roxanne laughed even harder. And then she blurted, "Boys suck."

We both laughed. "Amen to that," I said as I held up my Coke can in a toast, waiting for her to clink it with her chocolate milk carton. She did with little enthusiasm, but I smiled in satisfaction. It was a start. "It takes a cool person to know a cool person," I said.

The day dragged on, and no sign of Clark Anderson. Anywhere. Not until the end of Spanish class, right before lunch, when to my absolute horror I saw him, garbed in a new Punk Masters T-shirt and ripped jeans, leaning against the wall, talking to *Christina.*

When? How?

She wore a miniskirt with Uggs and a lime green, cropped T-shirt, blonde ringlets framing her face. And she was laughing. Like, so *deliberately.*

I turned and bolted in the opposite direction before he could see me. Considered cutting Study Hall.

No.

No way was I going to let Christina win.

Regardless of whether Clark was going to show up at Study Hall, regardless of whether he wanted to talk to Christina as she tripped over herself trying to get him to like her (and how *did* they get together? How did they meet?), I was going to strut through the hallway with my head held high. Like I *owned* this godforsaken school.

And strut I did. That is, until my shoe got caught on a wad of gum someone dropped on the floor, which made me trip and fall forward, drawing snickers from witnesses. I would've cried from the pain of scraping my knee had I not wanted to die of embarrassment. Nevertheless, I picked myself up and tried to stride on as if nothing happened. Except that I suddenly noticed that people were gawking at me. And when I entered my next class, a group of students in the back whispered things and glanced in my direction as they did. But no one said a word to me.

That couldn't be because of a klutzy fall.

Was I imagining things?

Finally, Study Hall. I inhaled deeply and approached the doorway.

Christina was waiting just outside the room.

"Hey, Wylie," she said in fake friendliness.

Already I could feel my steely resolve starting to shake.

"What do you want, Dickerson?" I said.

"Clark Anderson told me to tell you that he won't be coming to Study Hall today. In fact, I think he's going to run as fast and as far away from you as he can, now that he knows the truth," she said with a sneer.

"Whatever," I said, and entered the room, although I was dying to ask her to elaborate.

Christina wasn't about to let me have the last word, however, and followed me in, sitting in Clark's seat.

"Aren't you supposed to be somewhere else?" I asked.

"So tell me, what's it like?"

I looked at her like she was nuts. "What is *what* like?"

"Having a prostitute for a 'family friend.' I mean, that's not something you see every day."

Anxiety began to rumble in my stomach, like thunder looming in the distance and drawing closer. "What the *fuck* are you talking about?" I said the word loud enough to turn heads.

An evil, twisted, superior grin morphed onto Christina's face as she held up her phone in front of me. There, on her Facebook page, was the candid of David she'd snuck at IHOP, along with the caption: *And the truth comes out.* Underneath, in the first comment box, posted by Christina:

So now we know the truth. The mystery man in Wylie's life is a former male escort from New York City named Devin, not David.

A slew of other comments followed, asking how she knew and her explaining that she found out some girl's aunt's best friend *paid* him to go out with her and that he "was rather loved by the ladies," until I could only see random words like "whore" and "male slut" and "sick."

I dropped the phone and covered my mouth as I gasped.

"Hey!" said Christina as she bent down to pick it up. "Great, you cracked the screen. You are so buying me a new phone."

Next thing I knew, I lunged at Christina, screaming obscenities and knocking her to the floor, the contents of her purse erupting all over the place, phone screen completely shattering.

I felt hands on my elbows, trying to restrain me.

"That's my *father* you slammed, you lying *bitch!*" I screamed as I smacked her left and right. "*I hate you! I HATE YOU!!!*"

Christina was on the ground, her hands shielding her face, crying, and this time she wasn't feigning tears. I'd drawn blood.

Another teacher was called in, and I was yanked out of class and down to Mr. Berger's office. I ranted all the way, drawing looks from curious students and teachers as they either opened their doors to investigate the ruckus or closed them to block it out.

"You don't understand," I cried, temporary insanity taking over and making me forget that people could actually hear me. "She said things about my *father*. Spread *lies* about him! Invaded his privacy. *My* privacy."

"Tell it to Mr. Berger," said the teacher.

By the time I got to Berger's office, I was completely unhinged. I couldn't stop crying, couldn't speak, and couldn't breathe—I'd started to hyperventilate. One of the secretaries had to get a paper bag from the kitchenette in the teachers' lounge for me to breathe into.

Rather than let me calm down in the privacy of his office, Mr. Berger perpetuated my torture by making me sit in the waiting area for my mother to pick me up. Forty-five minutes later, she walked in, her hair coiffed the way I had done for her makeover, the thick black eyes replaced with softer, more neutral shadows, and she gasped the moment she saw me, ragged and tear-stained and holding the paper bag while I sobbed.

"What the hell happened?" she asked. I started to cry again as I stood up and buried my face in her shoulder. Mr. Berger stepped out, invited her into his office without me, and proceeded to explain.

My mother hit the ceiling. I could hear her as if the door was wide open. The secretaries all stopped what they were doing and looked in the direction of the office to listen.

Mom demanded to see Christina, threatening to knock the bitch out herself—her words. If I hadn't been in such a messed-up state I probably would've laughed. The door flew open and she pulled me up out of the chair. I don't think she meant to be so forceful, but I yelped.

"We're going, Wylie," she said. "We're getting you out of this school. My daughter is the victim of vicious rumors and bullying, and you punish *her*? Enough."

I kept my head down as she briskly took me out to the car while some of my classmates pointed their phones at me, just like one of those notorious celebrity criminals on their way to the courthouse. Once in the car, she took out her phone, tapped the touchscreen, and put the phone to her ear.

"Get over to the house *right now*," she said. "Both you and Andi."

David! She was calling David? Before Dad? Or maybe she'd called Dad before she came to the school.

David said something inaudible to me. "The shit hit the fan is what's wrong," she yelled. "Just get over here. Your daughter needs you." She disconnected without even waiting for him to say anything, tossed the phone back in her purse, started the car, and peeled out of the parking lot. She didn't cover more than a mile when she abruptly steered to the side of the road and put the car in park. She was breathing hard, as if she'd just run a marathon.

She undid her safety belt, scooted in her seat, and pulled me into her arms. I held on and cried. "Please tell me it isn't true," I pleaded, my face buried in her shoulder. "Please, please tell me they were all lies."

"Talk to your father," was all she said.

I had my answer.

Chapter Twenty-One

I shut myself in my room, unable to get Christina's words out of my head. *Male escort. Prostitute.*

I also couldn't stop kicking myself for outing David as my father in the midst of my tirade. I hadn't realized what I was saying while it was all happening, or to whom.

If Clark Anderson didn't hate me before all this, he most certainly hated me now, thanks to Christina. Plus I got suspended for attacking her once again and this time getting so violent that she bled (although I think it was from her phone cracking and shattering and her falling on it; then again, who knows what else she hit on the way down). The upside of suspension, however, was that I wouldn't have to face anyone in school tomorrow. Or ever again, if my mother was serious about not sending me back there.

David and Andi arrived about ninety minutes after my mom had called him—I saw their car pull into the driveway from my bedroom window. I parked myself at the top of the stairs once more and listened them talking downstairs—not hollering, but not quietly either. Trish came home and went straight upstairs, crying and consoling me as we went back to my room. She'd been affected by all this, too.

Another half hour later, David knocked on my door and identified himself. I let him in and Trish left to give us privacy.

"Hey," was all he said. I didn't reply.

My Sweet Sixteen party now felt like another lifetime ago. I remembered how it felt to leap into his arms and lose myself in his solid embrace. But in the present moment, all I could see was a phony. I was so *mad* at him, couldn't even look at him without those words ringing in my ears.

It occurred to me that this was the first time he'd ever seen my bedroom. He inspected the grape walls plastered with collages of photos of friends, cutouts from hairstyling magazines, and my paintings from art class before taking the desk chair and wheeling it over to the bed, like my dad usually does. *No*, I thought. *You are not my dad.* Then he sat and crossed one leg on top of the other.

He always looked so clean-cut and put together. Other than the day we met, I've never seen him with a hair out of place, or raggedy stubble, or smelling like anything other than a designer fragrance. Even now, he was garbed in dark blue jeans and a button-down shirt that definitely didn't come from Sears.

It was like we were meeting for the first time all over again.

"Your mom told me what happened at school," he finally said when I refused to speak. I wouldn't even say hello.

He waited for me to respond or even acknowledge him, but I maintained my stubborn ground. It was the only leverage I had.

He pressed on. "I am so, *so* sorry you found out this way. I never dreamed it would come out like this, especially via one of your classmates and someone who used to be your friend."

So, it was true.

I finally piped up. "You had plenty of chances to tell me yourself, but you didn't. Even yesterday in the car, you could've told me. But no. You had to wait for *the right time.*"

"You're right, Wylie. We totally fucked up. All four of your parents let you down."

I was surprised he cursed in front of me again, this time deliberately. It was also a little strange to hear the phrase "all four of your parents," although perhaps for the first time it sank in as truth. I had four parents now, and not one of them was less loving than the other. How could I have ever felt like I belonged to David and Andi? How could I ever think they compared to my real parents, were in some way better?

All I wanted right then and there was my dad. My *real* dad. Peter Baker. He was as real as fathers came.

"Were you a prostitute?" I asked.

It was time for him to come clean and he knew it. He seemed not to know where to start.

"Just dive right in," I said, remembering that piece of writing advice Andi had given me when I told her I had trouble writing introductions. Although I said it sarcastically rather than as encouragement. What did she know, anyway?

He heeded it, however, and after inhaling and exhaling a deep breath, did just that.

"Remember what I told you yesterday in the car, about my always wanting to prove to my father that I was a man, and that I made some morally questionable choices?"

I didn't nod or even shrug, so he continued, speaking in a matter-of-fact tone. "I was always entrepreneurial, so I started a business with a friend who had dropped out of college—not that that's relevant. His name was Christian. We were in our late twenties. He was in a lot of debt and wanted to make some quick cash. So the two of us decided to become escorts."

"What do you mean?"

"Do you know what an escort does?" he asked.

I shrugged.

"They get paid to go out with people. Female escorts get paid to go out with men; male escorts get paid to go out with women. At least that's how it traditionally works. It's like buying yourself a date to a party or a wedding or something like that. We'd conceived the idea as a hypothetical joke. Neither of us wanted steady girlfriends or wives and children, but we didn't want to be alone and hadn't gotten any dates in a while either, so we thought we'd kill two birds with one stone—get women to pay us to go out with them instead of the other way around, and make decent money without working too hard. Then we decided to do it for real. We had no idea how the escort business actually worked, nor did we do any research or work for another agency. We just made up our own rules as we went along."

"So what, exactly, did *you* do?"

"Christian and I hired ourselves out as dates for women, and we charged a lot of money."

"What's so bad about that?"

He began to wring his hands. "A lot of escorts are expensive because they do more than provide company."

I caught on. "Like, *sex*?"

"Yes," he replied, unable to look me directly in the eye.

"Like, prostitutes?"

"Some were, yes. Very upscale. They never referred to themselves as such, though. Just called themselves escorts."

"So, wait—you're saying *you* were one of them?"

He paused and took another deep breath before answering. "I had started out that way, yes."

Holy shit.

"What do you mean, you 'started out that way'?" I asked, becoming more belligerent by the second.

"Once the date part was over, I had sex with the women who hired me. But not long after the business took off, I stopped the sex part. Christian too. We made it a business policy. If sex happened, it wasn't part of the service, and it certainly wasn't part of the fee."

"Why?"

"For one thing, we didn't want to do anything illegal. For another thing, it was a line I just couldn't bring myself to cross anymore. It felt morally wrong. So we formed a company and hired other guys to be escorts as well, provided they didn't break the law either. It was all strictly on the level. We paid taxes and everything."

"But women still paid you to date them."

"Yes."

"But not to be their boyfriend."

"No, I tried not to let it get too personal."

The next thought that came to me made me cringe inside. *Oh. My God.* "You... and my mother... she *paid* you?"

"*No*," said David. "I was just starting out as an escort when I met your mother, but she wasn't a client. She and I went out as two regular people who were attracted to and liked each other."

"Did she know you were an escort?"

"Yes, she knew. She was working as a bartender at a hotel lounge in the city, and I was trying to drum up business."

"Did she offer you money?" I asked.

"*No*," he said even more emphatically than before.

"So you had sex because you both wanted to."

Wow. Here's a conversation most kids don't have with their parents. I had a feeling David was thinking the same thing.

"Yes," said David.

"On the first date?"

He nodded.

OK, so my mother wasn't sixteen when they'd done it, nor was she a virgin, probably. But still. *They did it on the first date. And she got pregnant as a result. Lovely.*

"So what happened after that?" I asked.

"She wanted to go out with me again. I wanted to keep on being an escort, however, and I wasn't very nice to your mom in the way I told her."

I had gleaned that much from my mother from early conversations. "No wonder she hates you," I said, not caring if I'd hurt his feelings. I pretty much hated him too.

He pressed on. "She was hurt, and she had every right to be."

I had suddenly gone from being revolted by David's sordid past to completely bewildered. What had made my mother go out with him, knowing beforehand what he did for a living? Had she fallen in love with David at first sight? Had she thought he'd been the one and she gotten it wrong? What if he'd had a different job?

I was quiet for some time, almost forgetting that he was sitting there. David finally interrupted my thoughts. "You OK?"

"Do you think that if you had gotten to know my mom, you would've fallen in love with her? Even married her?"

I remembered asking him this question early on when I'd found out he was my biological father. I'm not sure why I was asking him again, other than wondering if he would answer any differently.

"I honestly don't know," he said. "Maybe. I liked her a lot. I just didn't want to be in a relationship with anyone at the time, and I was more attracted to the money."

Nope. No differently. Except the part about the money. That was new information.

My thoughts then turned to Andi. I remembered what she had said during our Skype call about him treating her as "just another client," or something like that.

"What about Andi?" I asked.

"What about her?"

"Did *she* pay you to go out with her?"

179

"Andi and I met at a cocktail party. I was there with a woman she knew from her work."

"You mean you were with someone else who paid you."

"Yes," he replied.

"So how did you and Andi become friends?" I'd previously asked both of them that question too.

"We got to know each other."

"How?"

He hesitated again. "I think maybe you should ask her that one," he said, but changed his mind. Maybe he figured too much had been withheld from me already. "Andi and I had a special relationship. She... she wanted to be more comfortable in intimate situations with men. So I taught her how to do that, and in return she taught me all about writing and rhetoric, the stuff she teaches you, albeit at a more advanced level."

"You mean you tutored each other?"

"Pretty much," he said, and got that same faraway look that Andi gets when she talks about her past with David or Sam.

"So, was she a client, or wasn't she?"

"She started off as a different sort of client. The tutoring was a barter arrangement in lieu of her paying me. But she became much more to me. I just...I didn't know how to..." He trailed off, and stared at the floor. He didn't finish the story.

I felt as if everything I'd previously known about Andi was a lie. The two of them deserved each other.

I paused to process everything again.

"So let me see if I've got this," I said. "You used to get paid a lot of money to take women out on dates and have sex with them, and you called yourself Devin."

"I started out as an escort who also had sex, but stopped that part," he reiterated.

"During that time you met my mom, you went out and had sex on the first date, but *not* for money. That's when she got pregnant with me."

He nodded.

"For how long were you an escort?"

"A long time," he said. "Close to ten years, I think."

I couldn't picture what it would be like to date a different guy every night of the week for ten years, much less have sex with them.

"Did you go out with married women?" I don't know what made me think of that question.

He answered candidly, however. "Married women who were unhappy with their husbands, single women, women in high corporate positions who didn't have time to date but needed a 'plus one' for a special event, women who were socially awkward and didn't know how to attract a man on their own, women who just wanted to be pampered and paid attention to for a night...all kinds."

So he was a liar and an adulterer, and he got paid for it. My biological father, everyone!

"What made you quit?"

"I fell in love with Andi and didn't want to be with anyone else. I finally wanted to settle down and be in a serious relationship."

I remembered Saturday night at their house, when Andi and I were talking, how she said that David wasn't ready. It didn't make sense to me at the time but now I began to understand.

David looked sadder than I'd ever seen him. Lost, even. "By then she'd met Sam and wanted to be with him. I was heartbroken, but I knew she'd made the right decision for herself. I was still pretty much a mess at that time. My dad had just died, and I didn't know what else to do with my life. I didn't want to be Devin anymore, but I didn't really like who I was when I'd been David. And back then Andi didn't know the real me. Rather, she'd seen very little of the real me. I needed to take time off and figure it all out. I asked her to wait for me to get my life together, but she wasn't willing to do that. She wanted to move on. I couldn't blame her for that. And when I'd finally met Sam, I could tell in a manner of seconds that he was a good guy, and good for her. Her happiness meant more to me than my wanting us to be together."

Maybe he wasn't such a monster after all. After all, he changed, didn't he? And I knew he genuinely loved me and only wanted to do right by me. But how was I supposed to live with all this now? How was I supposed to go back to school and not be completely ashamed of or humiliated by him?

I went to the window and stared out, looking at the setting sun.

"Why didn't you want to tell me any of this?" I asked.

"People make judgments about escorts. Think it's just a fancy word for a hooker or a prostitute, which I suppose it is. I was afraid you'd think the worst of me, as would your friends if they ever found out."

Well, yeah.

"And maybe because I deserved it," he said. "I allowed women to use me, and I used them right back, although I always insisted I was just trying to make their lives better by making them feel special. It came at a very high price, however. Literally. I had never considered the long-term consequences. And your mother was afraid you'd judge her for going out with someone like me. We were both worried about what your friends would think of you, or what *you* would think of you."

"Well, I don't *hate* you," I said. I really didn't, I realized. His face softened with relief. "I am still mad and massively freaked out, though. It's weird to think you were this completely different guy with a different name doing... that stuff. But I really, *really* wish you'd told me. Then I wouldn't have gone all pitbull on Christina and gotten into so much trouble."

"We are all so sorry about what happened today. You didn't deserve that," said David.

"*You* should've told me," I scolded yet again. "All the horrible scenarios I've thought of. And the way I found out—coming from Christina—that was the awful part."

"How did she find out, anyway?"

I shrugged. "I guess it wasn't that hard. I mean, after all, I found you, didn't I?"

His eyes warmed and lightened.

We finally looked each other in the eye. "Now what?" I asked.

David stood up; he looked even taller than usual in my small bedroom. "Now we do damage control," he said with resolve.

"How?"

"We'll figure it out. Andi and I are going to stay nearby at a hotel tonight. We'll all meet in the morning to discuss it."

"I'm sorry for taking you away from your work responsibilities," I said. Not sure why.

"Don't be," he said. "I'd walk away from everything if you needed me to. *Everything.* And for the record, had I known your mother was pregnant, I would've quit being an escort in a New York minute."

God, how I wished he'd known! How different all our lives would have been if he had. Mom and David would've been married, and we wouldn't be living in stupid West Hartford. Maybe we'd live in Manhattan, or back on Long Island, and we'd be rich.

But then Mom wouldn't have met and married Dad, and David wouldn't have met and married Andi. I wouldn't have Trish for a sister or Roxanne and Bottsy for besties, and I never would've known Clark Anderson. He may hate my guts now, but it was worth these last four weeks of bliss to know him.

Maybe my life had turned out OK. Maybe the consequences of their actions weren't so bad after all.

183

"I vote we kick Christina's ass," I said.

"Is it wrong for me to second that?"

I laughed and shook my head.

"I really am sorry for all of this, Wylie," David said one last time.

"I know," I said. "Thanks, David."

We were back to formalities. For now. Maybe he and I would be OK too, eventually. Just like me and Roxanne, who texted me that night and vowed that Christina would never get away with it. We texted for an hour. Maybe something good came out of this after all.

Chapter Twenty-Two

It would've been so cool to live without Internet, to actually talk to people face to face without a smartphone glued to your hand. It would've been cool to hang out in record stores and watch a video like Michael Jackson's "Thriller" on TV for the first time ever. It would've been cool to write things down on paper all the time, and not feel compelled to tell the entire world that you're eating a banana.

Of course, I'd miss laptops, and it's way better to have all your music stashed in a phone than lugging around those massive Walkmans and tapes. But I'd be willing to trade my smartphone and laptop in for some privacy. Specifically, waking up and not finding out that half the kids in Study Hall took video of me mauling Christina, screaming about my father, and then posting it on Facebook for the entire world to see and share.

Because that happened.

No doubt it made its way to Clark too, who probably watched it and thought, *Yeah—cray-cray. Didn't see that one coming.* People I didn't know sent me friend requests and posted all kinds of comments, and the story now was that my mother paid David/Devin to have sex with her so she could get pregnant with me. I am the daughter of a male whore. Someone actually wrote that in reference to me. A *parent*, no less. I turned off Facebook Notifications and stayed off the Internet altogether. Picked up my Kindle Paperwhite and tried to concentrate on reading. The past few weeks I'd tried to read some of the books from Clark's reading list, but none of them held my interest. I hoped my not liking them wouldn't make me dead to him; then again, I already was, so what difference did it make? Instead I searched for books that interested *me*. That was one thing I liked about the Kindle—you could download a sample of any book for free. That way if you didn't like it, you didn't lose anything. Andi told me there was nothing wrong with going through twenty, even thirty samples before finding a book that interested me. It seemed to take me just that long, and I wondered if doing so made me extremely fussy or extremely clueless. Didn't real readers like to read no matter what was in front of them? I finally decided on a book about Vidal Sassoon, the revolutionary hairstylist. Maybe I'd ask my parents for book recommendations too. We could even start a family book club.

Mom refused to let Trish go to school the next morning, and of course I was suspended for attacking Christina. Trish actually wanted to go; she wanted to defend me, had been doing so ever since the stuff appeared online. My parents, however, were afraid of Trish winding up in a physical fight as well (to know Trish is to know that she takes shit from no one) and given that she was so close to graduation, they didn't want anything to jeopardize that. They stayed home from work as well, and David and Andi came over to discuss how to handle the viral posts. I was still reserved with David, and Andi too. I couldn't help it. It all took some getting used to, just like when I found out I had a biological father out there somewhere. It wasn't only the secret that had rattled me so much, but also the distortion of the picture—calling into question everything you've ever known about yourself and the people you love. Were you still the person you thought you were? Were they? It can drive you crazy sometimes, because then you can't trust anything you look at. Was

Clark ever the person I thought he was? Was Roxanne? Was Bottsy? Had Christina been the only person talking sense this entire time?

The words "cease-and-desist" came out of David's mouth, but whatever it meant, no one seemed to get behind it.

"Regardless of what legal steps we take," said Mom, "the real damage is done. People believe the story they want to believe. Wylie's reputation is ruined. *Our* reputations are ruined," she said to David.

"This is all my fault," I said. "I never should have let her get to me."

"This was not your fault," said Andi. "This was orchestrated by a bully."

"And I played right into it," I said. "I shouldn't have reacted the way I did. I didn't think about the consequences, just like always. I didn't think about anything at that moment. I just got so mad."

The doorbell rang. We all looked at each other, nonverbally asking whether we were expecting anyone.

"Maybe it's TMZ," I said. And then I burst into maniacal laughter. No one else joined me. They probably didn't know what TMZ was.

Trish answered the door, and then hollered for me from the foyer. Curious, I went to the door.

Bottsy stood inside the foyer, hands in his pockets, looking like he was about to give a speech in front of the entire school.

I could have cried. All I wanted to do was give him a big hug, but I stood in front of him mirroring his pose.

"Hey," I said. "Long time no see."

"Hey," he said, shifting his weight from foot to foot, his focus darting from me to the floor and back to me.

An excruciatingly awkward silence filled the space between us.

"You heard?" I finally said.

"Yeah," he answered. "For what it's worth, I totally blasted Christina for taking things too far. You have a lot more people on your side than you think. She got a lot of backlash for it."

"What did you say?"

"I told her she had no right to invade your privacy, and in such a trashy way. Called her a bully and a menace to the school—that second part might have been a little too harsh, but hey, she deserved it."

I chuckled. "Well, I think there's been enough trash talk, but thanks. It was nice of you to speak up for me, especially since I thought you were never going to speak to me again."

He looked as if I'd just shot him in the chest, and then went back to staring at his shoes. "I'm sorry, Botts, I didn't mean it like that. I…"

"Can we go outside and talk for a minute?" he asked.

We stepped outside, traipsed to the driveway, and both leaned our backs against his mom's blue Prius. He must have gotten his junior license already. He and Roxanne and I had made a pact that we would all give each other a ride first as soon as we got our licenses. I wonder who got the first ride instead of us.

"I'm sorry I dropped out on you like that," he started. "I was embarrassed. I couldn't bring myself to face you again. Or Rox."

"When?" I asked. "I mean, for how long have you… when did it start?"

"The night we kissed. It was so awkward and weird, but I couldn't stop thinking about it. And then I realized I had liked it, and, well… I guess I realized that I liked you."

I paused for a second before responding. "I'm sorry," I said. "It's not that I didn't like it. I just didn't feel the same way. I wanted you as a friend. And I know how shitty a feeling that is, when someone you like doesn't like you that way. It kills me to hurt you that way."

"Yeah, I know. Kills me to hurt Roxanne that way too."

"Just so you know, I had *no clue* she liked you that way. She never said a word to me. Had I known, I probably would have tried to push the two of you together."

"God, Wylie, it's all such a mess. I'd give anything for the three of us to go back to being the way we used to be, before we all got hormones and shit."

I laughed, and he echoed it.

"Playing Space Team on our phones at lunch…" I started.

"Beating your asses at Sorry when we were kids…" he countered.

"You hogging all the chocolate chips when Roxanne and I baked cookies."

"You hogging the back seat of the car when you and Rox came with us to Mystic."

"I did not!" I playfully argued.

"Please. The only thing that kept me from being pushed out the door was my seatbelt. I still have the strap mark branded across my chest."

We cracked up. And then we became silent and sad just as quickly.

"I'd give anything—*anything*—to be back in that car," he said. I knew what he meant.

"Do you think we ever will?" I asked.

"I don't know. I finally spoke to Rox a couple of days ago. Couldn't face her for a while either. Not just because I was embarrassed, but I was so pissed at her for the way she just up and outed me like that. I mean, I get that she was hurting, but still."

"Yeah, I know. It massively sucks when someone announces your business to the world. But don't be too hard on her. It's not like she was doing it to deliberately be mean to you. I don't think she was even deliberately being mean to me. It's just that sometimes you say and do the dumbest things to the people you love most, all because deep down you're afraid of losing them."

My mother's words had finally made sense to me. She'd been afraid of losing me, and had made a choice not to deceive me, but to protect what she wanted to hold on to. So did David. It didn't make them bad people. It just meant they'd made mistakes. And the same was true for me with Clark. I was desperate to hold on to the thing I wanted most.

"What's up with you and Wonder Boy?" Bottsy blurted, as if he'd just read my mind. Before I could answer, he laughed nervously. "Sorry, that was mean. It wasn't deliberate." He winked and nudged my arm with his elbow.

I playfully punched him back. But the thought of Clark made my heart sag, as if weighted by a bag of rocks. "He went M.I.A.," I said. "I haven't seen or heard from him since this whole thing went down. But things kind of blew up between us on Friday, so I wasn't really expecting to."

"What happened?" he asked.

I shook my head as if trying to make sense of it. "I went berserk, I guess. Jumped in too soon or something."

"That hardly seems like a good enough reason not to support you at a time like this."

"Maybe he doesn't know," I said even as the image of Christina talking to him rammed itself to the front of the line of my thoughts.

"Everyone knows, Wylie."

"Lovely."

"Look, I'm just saying. As weird as things have been between us, there was no way I was going to sit back and let you go through this alone. We're friends. I want us always to be friends." He paused. "Do you think that's possible? Do you think we'll be able to get there again?"

"I honestly don't know," I said. "But I hope so. I want to. I've missed you, Botts." And then I began to cry. "I really, really missed you," and went straight into his arms, where we hugged for a long time.

When we finally let go, he asked, "So what are you going to do about all this?"

"No clue. We're all discussing it inside. My parents. David. Andi. Me. It's so insanely awkward."

"So, it was true?"

I nodded. "Not the part about my mother paying him. They went out on a legitimate date. But yeah, he was an escort. He's not anymore. He hasn't been in a long time."

"Don't let her get away with it," he said of Christina. "And don't let *him* get away with it either." I knew to whom he was referring.

Bottsy and I hugged again, and he promised he'd text me later. I stood in the driveway and watched him drive away before retreating to the house.

"Everything OK?" asked Mom when I returned to the kitchen.

"Yeah," I said and smiled. "Or at least I think it will be."

David and Andi didn't stay much longer. There really wasn't anything anyone could do but let it all blow over. Or at least, we couldn't think of anything else to do.

That night, I thought about what Bottsy had said about Clark. *Why? Why hasn't he texted or visited me? Why didn't he write me a letter? Why didn't he come to Study Hall that day? Why did he bail when I needed him most?*

An idea came to me.

I knocked on my parents' bedroom door. Dad beckoned me in. Mom was sitting at her vanity and applying face cream. Dad was sitting on the bed with his tablet.

"What's up?" said Dad.

"I think I should write a letter," I said.

"To whom?" asked Mom.

"I don't know. Like, the entire school. I mean, I should post it on Facebook or something."

"You mean like an open letter?" said Dad.

"Yeah, I guess so. That way I can regain control of the situation and set a few details straight."

"Be careful, Wylie," said Mom. "Sometimes that can backfire."

"Well, it depends on how I write it. I mean, I have to consider my audience and focus on making a logical appeal rather getting sucked into the emotions and shocking people."

Wow. Andi's rhetorical lessons were finally paying off. I couldn't help but be grateful at the moment.

"I'd like to at least try," I said. "I'll show it to you when I'm done. You both can have final approval. If you don't like it, then I won't post it."

"OK," said Dad. "We trust you."

We trust you. If only they knew how much those words meant to me. How long it had been since I believed them.

"Thank you," I said. I went back to my room, took out my laptop, and began to write.

Chapter Twenty-Three

I wrote it all out longhand in my notebook first, nonstop, letting it all spill out onto the page regardless of whether it made sense or was organized or correct, just like Andi had taught me. That alone took me well over an hour. It was strangely satisfying, like punching your pillow or running laps. Then I went to bed and left it on my desk. Andi had taught me to do that too, to "let it marinate," as she called it.

The next day, I re-read it and crossed most of it out, writing in the spaces between the lines or on both left and right margins with arrows pointing to where the new passages should go. I thought about my audience: who would be reading this? Roxanne and Bottsy? Christina? Caitlyn and Hillary and Annette and everyone else who came to my party? I mentally removed Roxanne and Bottsy from the list—sure, they would read it, but there wasn't anything in there that they didn't already know, and I'd have their support no matter what. It was really for those people who'd Friended me but hadn't acted like a friend lately.

I continually made changes as I typed, and read it out loud (something else Andi had taught me) before finally printing it out, even though it still wasn't the final copy, and showing it to my parents. They both sat on my bed, Mom passing each page to Dad as she read them.

"Where did you get the idea to do this?" asked Mom.

"From Martin Luther King, I guess" I said.

"It's very well written," she said.

I smiled. I guessed all the letters I'd written to Clark had paid off.

"I think it shows who the more mature person is," said Dad. He put his arm around me and pulled me to him.

"Thank you, Dad," I said. "That means a lot to me."

"You should probably give it to Andi for editing," said Mom. "Just to make sure it's perfect."

I was so shocked I almost fell off my chair. My mother was actually *encouraging* me to go to Andi for help?

"I think I'll send it to my teacher instead," I said, wheeling the chair back to my desk and looking for Mr. Fischetti's email address. Maybe I was still a little mad at Andi too. Or maybe it was just time for me to reach out to others.

"Send it to them anyway," said Mom. So I did.

All that work took my mind off the fact that I still hadn't heard from Clark.

Two hours later, David called me. "I read your letter," he said. "It made me very proud." His voice broke on the last word. I wanted to still be mad at him, but I just couldn't. Not at that moment, when he was *proud* of me. Not when he was reaching out. Besides, I'd had enough of Clark's cold shoulder. Why should I put anyone else through that?

"Do you think it'll make a difference?" I asked.

"It will make a difference in *you*," he said.

I paused. "David, I know I've been a little standoffish with you since… since finding everything out. I'm really sorry."

"It's OK, *carina*," he said. "You have every right to be." Then he added, "Can I still call you that?"

"Of course you can," I replied. "I like it when you do."

"Good, because I like doing it. By the way, Andi found two typos in your letter. OK if she sends you the corrections?"

"Sure," I said. "I don't think I would've gotten the idea to do it had she not sent me that 'Letter from Birmingham Jail' or taught me those appeals."

"I'll tell her you said so," he said.

"No," I said, "I'll tell her. Next time we Skype."

The following morning, I changed my Facebook profile photo to one of David and me from his wedding on New Year's Eve. Rather than copy and paste the entire text into a status update, I saved the file as a PDF, then saved each PDF page as a JPEG, making sure the pages were clearly numbered. I then posted each one to my Facebook page with a title: *Letter from Wylie Jean Baker.*

> *On two recent, separate occasions, Christina Dickerson and I had confrontations. The first confrontation was initiated by me, when I poured a can of Coke on her head. I never apologized for it, so I want to now say that I'm sorry for doing something so stupid. The second confrontation resulted in me pushing Christina to the floor, hitting her, and breaking her phone. And while I do not defend my behavior, I want to explain what provoked it.*
>
> *Approximately two months ago, Christina posted a photo of a man she met at my Sweet Sixteen party and asked people for information about him. She posted this photo and asked for this information without his knowledge, permission, or regard for his privacy.*
>
> *That man is my biological father.*
>
> *The man who raised me, Peter Baker, is my father. He*

adopted me as his own when I was three years old, and he has done an outstanding job as a father, never once leading me to believe that I was anyone other than his daughter, and he loves me very much. I, in return, love him very much.

However, when I discovered he wasn't my biological father, I set out to find the man who was, and was successful. Last September I met him, and since then he and I have cultivated a special relationship. In an age where so many kids come from broken homes and have two sets of parents, I'm fortunate to be among them, and I love both in different ways.

I did not tell my friends about my biological father for two reasons. One, I wasn't ready to, and two, he and my mother asked me not to. My biological father also asked me not to post photos of him on Facebook. Several of my friends noticed the resemblance at my party even though we were both in costume. They asked who he was, but I didn't tell them. Christina decided to get answers without me, and eventually found out that my father, David, at one time worked as an escort in New York City. Without asking him or me to confirm, or producing evidence to support these allegations, Christina revealed this information on her Facebook page. She then used the information to taunt me. That is what prompted my attack on her.

I was wrong to use violence. I recently learned about Martin Luther King, Jr. and his nonviolent civil rights movement. He strongly believed that the response to violence had to be nonviolence, and that justice must be won nonviolently. In no way am I comparing myself to the civil rights movement, nor do I hold myself anywhere near Dr. King's character. But he taught me the importance of using words as a means of persuasion. He also taught me that you cannot overcome a bully by acting like a bully. That's why I regret attacking Christina the way I did, and why I accept the consequences of my actions, a week's suspension from school.

If you want to know who I am, then talk to me yourself. But if you post a comment on someone's page making a judgment about someone you don't know, have never even met, don't even know what she looks like, then you are no better than the bully. If you want to know about my biological father, then ask him. As for what he did in the past, that is his business and his past. Today he is a successful businessperson in the art world, is sensitive and thoughtful, and loves his wife and daughter very much. He has only known me for less than a year, but he has acted as if he has known me all his life.

One of the rumors that circulated about me is that I was the product of a union in which my mother paid my father to get pregnant. Without knowing my mother or David, without a shred of proof, and without a single care for the daughter their union produced, people made this claim using hurtful, judgmental words. THIS RUMOR IS ONE HUNDRED PERCENT FALSE. My mother and David dated, and then they went their separate ways like so many other couples out there.

Once again, I would like to apologize for my actions. It won't happen again. But I ask you all to please consider your actions as well. Language is a powerful tool. Like any other tool, it must be used safely. My generation doesn't use words anymore. We use abbreviations, symbols, emojis, and "Like" to communicate. We post pictures of ourselves going through life instead of conversing with people about our lives. Thanks to writing letters, I learned more about one person in a few short weeks than some people I've known for years. If I'm going to use words, and participate in the process of writing, I want to use them in ways that don't hurt people. Christina's actions were wrong, and I will not allow her to make unsubstantiated claims about me. But I also don't want to treat her the way she treated me.

    Sincerely,
    Wylie Jean Baker

Within thirty minutes, the three pages received twenty Likes. I refused to read the comments, knowing that some would be from haters. David was right—it wasn't about making a difference in them as much as it was about making a difference in me. And it did.

Roxanne texted me: *OMG u r awesome!!!!* Funny how I could no longer stand the letter abbreviations for words. Stupid, snooty Clark Anderson and his texting grammar rules.

Bottsy followed: *You said it way better than I did. :)*

It felt so good to have Roxanne and Bottsy back, even though I knew it would be a while before the three of us hung out together again, if ever.

That night at bedtime, my phone pinged just as I was about to turn off the light. Figuring it was Roxanne, I took it from my bedside table and looked at the screen.

Well done, Wylie Baker.

My heart ached so badly when I saw the words, imagining his sparkling eyes behind them.

I considered ignoring it. Put the phone back on the table. But ten minutes of staring at a dark ceiling was enough torture.

I texted back: *Thank you, Clark Anderson.* Then I silenced my phone and went to sleep.

He didn't text back.

Chapter Twenty-Four

I always wondered what it would be like to be the star of a reality show and have cameras follow you everywhere. Now I know. Sort of. Because that's exactly what it felt like when I returned to school— people who never gave me the time of day now gawked at me as they passed me in the hallway or sat in class, and people who had once been friendly with me but had succumbed to Christina's reign of terror now avoided eye contact at every turn, wearing masks of guilt and contrition. Although, come to think of it, maybe they weren't masks. Maybe those were their real faces.

Regardless, I felt like a caged animal at a zoo the day I returned to school following my suspension, on display for everyone to ogle and pity and stick out their hands for a petting or a scrap of food.

So far I'd made it through half the day, scaling hurdle after hurdle— the stares, whispers, and face-to-face comments from classmates. Christina and I avoided each other like we were contagious.

One hurdle remained, the highest one yet: Clark Anderson.

Placing bets on whether Clark was going to show up to Study Hall was a gamble I wasn't willing to make. The odds were fifty-fifty. I sat at my desk, tapping my foot incessantly, until he walked in just as the bell rang, avoiding eye contact with everyone, myself included, looking more somber and serious than I'd ever seen him.

He sat next to me. "Hey, Wylie," he said, forcing friendliness, like I had done with Roxanne.

God, I was so nervous I thought I would pass out. "I wasn't sure you'd show," I said.

"Graduation," he said. "I want out. Can't afford to take risks."

"Yeah, I know."

That awkward, unbearable, makes-you-feel-like-you're-naked-on-TV, lasts-for-seconds-but-feels-like-hours silence passed between us. Even worse than the one between me and Bottsy the previous week.

He reached into his backpack and pulled out a folded sheet of paper.

"Sooo," he said, "I wrote you a letter…"

Something in me snapped. "No," I said. "I don't want a *letter*." I tried to keep my voice down. "I want you to *explain* right here and now why you didn't call, text, or come by my house to make sure I was OK. Sure, I acted like a love-obsessed idiot and had a colossal meltdown, but still. I thought you cared about me."

"I do care about you," he said softly. I could hear the hurt in his voice.

"Then explain it to me," I repeated. "Right here, right now."

He shook his head and darted left and right. "Too many eyes and ears."

"Then let's get out of here."

"How?" he asked.

I gathered my things and motioned for him to follow my lead. I approached Mrs. Lewis at her desk.

"Everything OK, Wylie?" she asked.

"I'm a little dizzy," I said in a weary voice (although I didn't have to pretend much). "Can Clark take me down to the nurse?"

She signed a Hall Pass for Clark and me, and we walked out.

"Now what?" he said.

"Well, we can't cut for the rest of the day, not when I've already missed a whole week and you're so close to graduating. And we can't go to the art room either right now. That's normally where I hide out when it's not being used."

"I know where we can go," he said. "It's outside, kind of a blind spot where no one will see us from any doors or windows."

He led me out a side door and toward the back of the school; there we stood in the shade of the corner where two brick façades met.

"So?" I started.

He took a deep breath. "First of all, I feel like a massive tool for not being there for you when all that shit went down with Christina and everyone finding out about your father. I can't imagine what that was like for you."

"You mean you *were* a massive tool. You could have asked me what it was like. I would have then told you that it more than sucked. But you didn't. All I got was some flimsy little text from you. That's it. Nothing. You know how you're always joking that I'd be dead to you if I don't like your stupid books or baseball team? Well, that's how I felt."

"You didn't exactly pick up the phone either after it happened," he said.

"Why should I? You weren't talking to me. I figured you wrote me off as Texty McStalkerson and wanted nothing more to do with me."

He cracked up and practically doubled over. "Sorry, Wylie, but that was really funny," he said when he composed himself. He turned sad in an instant. "God, I've missed laughing with you."

"I am sorry for that, by the way," I said. "That's not who I really am. I…I was just really scared to lose you, and I didn't think about the consequences of my actions."

"I'm sorry too. I guess I just needed time to sort through it all. Thing is, with graduation and college coming down the pike so fast, I just don't think my getting involved with you or anyone else is a good idea. But I don't want to lose you either. I know it's such a cliché to say let's just be friends, but I really want that."

Did you hear that *splat*? It was my heart, popping out of my chest and splattering all over my Chucks like a water balloon filled with goop.

"I can't do that, Clark," I said. "I mean, I still don't want to lose you, but how can I go back to being just friends when I'm in—" I cut myself off.

Clark refused to make eye contact and leaned against the wall.

"I'm trying to protect you, Wylie."

"No, I think you're trying to protect yourself." He didn't respond. I paused for a beat before adding, "And what did Christina tell you that day? I saw the two of you together."

"Nothing," he said. "It was stupid."

"She told you about David, right? Figured you didn't know either?"

"It was weird, all right? I didn't know what to think. I'm all confused, Wylie. I don't know what I want."

At that moment I didn't know what I wanted either. I thought it would be a no-brainer. But how could I expect to have any kind of relationship with Clark if he was so unavailable? And not just because he was leaving for college in a month. Writing letters was supposed to be a way to reveal more about ourselves, but I suddenly wondered if he was really using them to hide.

Another ridiculously awkward block of silence ticked away.

"You'd better get back to Study Hall," I said, staring at my feet.

"What about you?"

"I'll go to the nurse. I really could do with lying down and closing my eyes for a few minutes. This day has lasted a week."

"Well, can I at least walk you there?"

"Why torture the both of us?" I said. "Your indecision is actually a very clear decision. You're either all in or you're not. I'm not good with maybes."

"I'm really sorry, Wylie."

"Me too," I said.

We re-entered the school and I waved in lieu of a verbal goodbye as we parted in opposite directions.

Maybe I had resigned myself to the situation—Clark Anderson didn't want me. Or rather, he wanted a less-complicated college experience more. Like Andi had once said, sometimes something could be right, but things get in the way. Life was just plain unfair sometimes. It was how I responded to it that mattered, choosing—no, *daring*—to live my life without Clark Anderson. Maybe I could, and it would still be a good life.

Finally, I felt sixteen. As if it had forgotten my birthday and showed up late. It felt good.

Chapter Twenty-Five

June

Mom, Dad, and I sweated as we sat on metal folding chairs on the high school football field in eighty-degree sunshine. We'd already applied sunscreen twice (they were grateful to me for having the presence of mind to bring it), and loaned the tube to nearby families who were turning red. The rose in my lap was starting to wilt from thirst.

Trish had lost the argument with Mom to wear shorts and a tank top underneath her cap and gown, and instead was baking in the sundress she bought when the two of us went on a recent shopping spree. I, too, sported a flower-print sundress along with matching colored flip-flops, also products of said shopping spree. I wore my hair in a bun, seriously considering chopping it all off for the summer into a pixie cut and donating the excess to one of those places that makes wigs for women with cancer, in honor of Andi's mother.

Principal Nunan spoke first. Then Melissa Streit, Class President. Then Craig Keisling, Valedictorian. Everyone said the same thing: graduation wasn't an ending but a beginning; the time had come to go out in the world; fond memories and looking back someday at the greatest years of our lives.

Good God, I hoped not. If these were the greatest years of my life, then I was in for quite a shitty life.

It was a bummer that the only two names I wanted to hear came at the very beginning of the alphabet and I'd be stuck sitting through the rest of the ceremony. I'd tried to convince my parents to go out for coffee or something in the meantime and then coming back for Trish, but no dice. At least I had my phone with me, and I texted with Roxanne throughout most of the speeches and the diploma ceremony.

Do you see him? she texted.

Not yet, I replied.

I waited with bated breath, trying to get a glimpse of him among the sea of maroon and gold caps and tassels and sashes. Clark and I had no choice but to see each other in Study Hall, and even though we still sat together, it was as if we'd forgotten how to talk to each other, or had run out of things to say. As if without letters, we'd been strangers all along. I hated it, but I had no idea how to fix it.

Mr. Berger—a man who was about as useful as his necktie—called out the name: *Clark Anderson.*

I watched the lanky figure slouch across the stage, his Transitions lenses shading his eyes, the shock of inky hair also hidden under the cap. He took the diploma and shook hands with the principal in a lackluster manner, as if this was all some rote exercise he was goaded into. But then he put his feet together and took an exaggerated bow in front of Mr. Berger. The audience cheered, and in return he blew a kiss to them. Weeks of trying to convince myself I was over him came undone in the instant of that bow and kiss.

Mom put her arm around me, and leaned in. "He is cute," she said, watching him on the video screen above.

"I know," I replied sadly.

Minutes later, when Mr. Berger called out: *Patricia Baker*, Mom, Dad, and I stood up and wooted for her. She turned in our direction and craned her neck and waved as she received her diploma. I caught the whole thing on my phone. When I looked at Dad, I could tell he was choked up. I recognized a look in his eyes that I'd seen in

206

David's when it came to me. I was glad to know that look, to be able to recognize it, even if I couldn't describe it.

I felt close to her at that moment in ways I hadn't expected.

When the Class of 2014 finally turned their tassels and tossed their caps into the air, I jumped out of my seat and bee-lined towards the graduates before they could reunite with their parents, pose for pictures, and head for the parking lot and restaurants of their choice to celebrate.

I bumped and zigzagged my way through, the urgency increasing with each passing second. Step by step, beat by beat.

I didn't know why I was doing what I was about to do, why I felt the need to. Maybe I was holding out one last hope. Maybe I was delusional. Or maybe I didn't want him to leave West Hartford thinking I didn't love him anymore.

I froze when I saw him.

He was standing with a few buddies, taking selfies, when I called his name.

He whisked around and saw me, startled. Either his buddies didn't know me or pretended not to. They gave Clark a friendly nod and a "See ya later," and Clark gestured the same in return.

I pointed at him as if I'd suddenly recognized him. "Clark Anderson," I said. "Class of 2014."

He imitated my stance. "Wylie Baker," he replied. "In a class of her own."

I smiled. He smiled back.

"Looking for your sister?" he asked.

"No, I was looking for *you*." He seemed surprised by this admission. "I would've come today even if Trish hadn't graduated," I added. He took notice of my sincerity.

"You look really pretty," he said.

My heartbeat did a drumroll.

"You too—I mean," I caught myself and broke into an embarrassed giggle, "you look good. Happy to finally be done with this place."

"You have no idea." Then he changed his mind. "Actually, you do."

I suddenly remembered the rose in my hands. "This is for you," I said as I extended it to him. "A reminder of Elizabeth Park. Sorry it's a little wilted. It's hotter out here than I thought it was going to be today."

He took the rose and looked at it as if he'd never seen one before.

"Congratulations, Clark. You're going to have a wonderful time at Edmund College. Best of all, you're going to be free."

He remained fixated on the flower. "No one's ever given me a rose before. In fact, no one's ever given me a flower of any kind."

"I guess most guys don't get them. It's usually the other way around."

"Thanks, Wylie. It was very thoughtful of you."

My heart felt like it was going to pummel through my chest any moment and splat on the ground. I began to tremble as emotion started to build like a crest of a wave about to break.

"Well, see you," I said.

I turned and started to walk away when I heard him call out, "I miss you, Wylie Baker!"

I flung around to find him taking steps toward me, his arms already extended. I rushed him and landed in his arms; he lifted me off my feet and spun me around.

I clasped my hands around his neck, and didn't let go. Neither did he.

"I've missed you so badly," he said. "And I'm so sorry I wasn't there for you. I should have been. I should've stood in front of you. I was such a coward."

And then he kissed me.

It was the best kiss of my life—so warm and wet and perfect. I felt like I was floating on air, until I realized I was, literally—he'd lifted my feet off the ground. I clasped my arms around his neck and ran my fingers through the ends of his hair, damp with sweat. We kissed again and again and again. And when we finally finished, our foreheads touched, and he said with a voice that only I could hear, "I love you, Wylie Baker."

The words somehow put the entire world into perfect alignment.

"I love you too, Clark Anderson."

Chapter Twenty-Six

July

Clark and I stood next to Oliver, packed to the brim, and we held each other for what felt like hours. I wished I could bottle the scent of him. He let me keep one of his Punk Masters T-shirts.

Finally, he let go. "It's time," he said.

"Do you have everything?" I asked.

"I do," he said.

"Do you have the drawing?"

He pointed to the front passenger seat. There occupied the self-portrait I had been working on ever since that first day he showed up in Study Hall and asked me to do a drawing for him. For hours I sat posed in front of a full-length mirror, one leg crossed in front of the other, knee pointing upward, and a slight three-quarter point-of-view.

"I'll never let it go," he said. "It's my most prized possession now."

"You're going to have an amazing time at college. I just know it."

"And you're going to get through the next two years of high school intact, no matter where you end up. You'd better tell me all about it."

"You know I will."

We kissed and embraced each other and touched foreheads one last time.

"Goodbye, Wylie Baker," he said.

"Until we meet again," Clark Anderson, I replied. "I love you."

"I love you back."

He got into his car and started it, looked behind him as he pulled out of my driveway, slowly rolled up the street. I remained where I was until I could no longer see his car. Then I went inside and up to my room.

Acknowledgments

I wrote the bones of this book during NaNoWriMo (National Novel Writing Month) in 2013, months before the release of *She Has Your Eyes*. When I completed and submitted it for publication, editors and agents had difficulty "placing" the book into the market. Love, Wylie seemed to fit neither into the Young Adult box nor its predecessors' Women's Commercial Fiction/Contemporary Romance boxes. I had then decided to self-publish, but industry advisors discouraged me, cautioning that I could "confuse" my audience with a teenage protagonist, even though she spun-off from one of my most popular novels.

Thus, I decided to indefinitely shelf *Love, Wylie*. And I've regretted it ever since.

I loved Wylie, and when I occasionally took out the manuscript and read it, I loved this story, loved the possible directions it could travel, and loved seeing David and Andi again. And when I recently shared an excerpt on my personal Facebook page, the feedback was resoundingly the same.

Five years later, I decided to listen to that love instead of convention (I've never been conventional anyway) and bring Wylie into the world again.

My gratitude goes to the following:

Pamela Mottola and K.D. Guadagno, who beta-read the story very early on and helped me smooth over the plotholes.

Developmental editor extraordinaire Tiffany Yates Martin, who always helps me take my work from manuscript to finished novel with patience, humor, and determination.

Copy editor Jim Thomsen, who helped me refine the language and encouraged an extra story detail or two, all for the better.

Jovana Shirley, who formatted the book for digital reading.

Countless readers, past and present, who have kept David and Andi alive and welcomed Wylie into their hearts.

My Billings friends and community who gave me so much more than a home.

The Undeletables, who well, still haven't deleted me.

My families—the Lorellos, Lancasters, and Clineses—who love me as much as I love them.

Spatz, who kept me company while my husband was away on all those pipeline jobs.

And last but never least, my wonderful husband, Craig Lancaster, who designed the fabulous cover, prepared the book for publication, and housed it under his independent imprint, Missouri Breaks Press. He supported this project one hundred percent, and sacrificed much of his own writing life in 2017 to allow mine to continue. Every day with my best friend, business partner, and fellow traveler is a cherished gift.

About the author

Elisa Lorello is a Long Island native, the youngest of seven children. She earned her bachelor's and master's degrees at the University of Massachusetts Dartmouth and taught rhetoric and writing at the college level for more than ten years. In 2012, she became a full-time novelist.

Elisa is the author of eight novels, including the bestselling *Faking It*, a memoir, and a book about writing. She has been featured in *Montana Quarterly* and *Rachael Ray Every Day* magazines, and Jane Friedman's blog series 5 On. She also was a guest speaker at the Triangle Association of Freelancers 2012 and 2014 Write Now! conferences. In May 2016, she presented a lesson for the Women's Fiction Writers Association spring workshop. She continues to speak and write about her publishing experience and teach the craft of writing and revision.

Elisa enjoys reading, walking, Nutella, and all things Duran Duran. She plays guitar badly and occasionally bakes. She lives with her husband, bestselling author Craig Lancaster.

On Facebook: Elisa Lorello, Author
On Twitter: @elisalorello
Subscribe to elisalorello.com and receive exclusive updates, offers, and gifts!

Don't miss the other books featuring these characters

FAKING IT	ORDINARY WORLD	SHE HAS YOUR EYES
Elisa Lorello's debut novel, a worldwide bestseller	*The compelling sequel, continuing Andi and David's story*	*The introduction of Wylie Baker into the series*

www.ingramcontent.com/pod-product-compliance
Lightning Source LLC
Chambersburg PA
CBHW051249250626
47155CB00009B/3228